WIDOW'S DOZEN

MAREK WALDORF

WIDOW'S DOZEN

TURTLE POINT PRESS

NEW YORK

PUBLISHED BY TURTLE POINT PRESS

WWW.TURTLEPOINTPRESS.COM

COPYRIGHT © 2014 BY MAREK WALDORF

ALL RIGHTS RESERVED

ISBN 978-1-933527-77-2

LCCN 2012949794

PRINTED ON ACID-FREE, RECYCLED PAPER

IN THE UNITED STATES OF AMERICA

to Helen

BEFORE

OTHERWISE

TOO LATE

BEFORE

FETCH

Truth was there could be no question of her responsibility for Aaron's death. Murder, that's something else again. Murder involves intent, and can a dumb animal actually possess the "intent to kill"? Ridiculous, right? But in fact I don't know what to think anymore. The more outlandish the idea appears, the more effort I seem to put into believing it. Because there she is—preventing me from sleeping, observing me as I do my best to understand.

Why? Revenge. Sheer malevolence. No reason. So why do I keep her?

In one sense, there's nothing simpler to cope with than loss. The more I feel it, the less complicated it seems, and the routines that constitute my day-to-day existence—the commute, the practice, endless chores, the downtime in front of the TV, the walks—all have become unlikely emanations of that simplicity, the obstinate abstractness death holds over me. So she eyes me, so what? So she won't let me sleep because she has a guilty conscience. So what does she want from *me*? Just listen.

We first met during the winter of my sophomore year. My college roommate, a new recruit to the then-burgeoning Church of Christ, had invited me to join him and his born-again cohorts on a few weekend runs to Greek Peak near the Cortlands. It was a package deal, and a good enough one, I figured, to make allowances for the company I'd be keeping. For some reason, Aaron joined us on the second trip. He was riding shotgun, and he was doing everything in his power to make a bad impression—which he did, on me. The Church of Christers were going out of *their* way to show how unflappable they were. He talked a lot of puerile blasphemy. Failing to get a rise, he started in with his sexual hangups. It was like a one-man Truth or Dare session, and I can't remember who repelled me more, this petty maestro of needling and put-upon resentment, or his hosts for not chucking him out of the car.

Our paths crossed again several months later, at a

party. To my surprise, he remembered me—just not my name. I feigned ignorance, then amnesia. It wasn't long before I realized that he had nobody else to converse with, and since I was in the same boat (abandoned by my date), I decided to stick it out with him for a while. I had to admit he was more of a character than I'd given him credit for.

He was also older than most of us, by about five years. He wanted to make me understand that his association with the Church of Christ had been entirely opportunistic—he'd been writing an exposé on them for *Pipe Dream*, Harpur's weekly paper—and while not outright implausible, something in the story or his telling of it tilted me toward disbelief. Aaron had a habit of inventing complexities where none were needed. A ferociously dignified liar. Besides, around the time of Aaron's purported tenure, I'd "comped" for the paper—unsuccessfully, in fact—and would have remembered him. Later, for that reason or a different one, I hinted that he was full of shit. He pretended he himself *couldn't* be needled.

"Exactly what part of the country did you say you're from?"

* * *

Not too long into law school, the same place as I'd gone undergrad, I saw I had made a terrible mistake. Out of what I thought was a lack of options, I'd chosen a career I had neither the aptitude nor the inclination for. The "law" of course can be made to cover many interests. Friends and family advised me to identify a niche. I tried corporate, criminal, taxes, torts and international before I made housing my area, not because it was the most interesting, but it seemed the easiest to coast through. It was around this time that I started running into Aaron more often. The third or fourth time, it occurred to me that these encounters might not be the product of chance.

So this was where our friendship began, queasily but in earnest. Since I lived near his job and was rarely out, he would drop by after work, in the early evening, and wind up staying late. We watched a lot of TV together, during which Aaron kept up a running sarcastic commentary—I've never met anybody with such a mania for attaching points to things. He left his background sketchy: mother dead (his mixed-up guilt and sorrow were "unimaginable") and "an egregious lump" of a dad, whom he never saw anymore and swore he'd kill, obviously hyperbolizing, if he did.

He could fall into free-form, all-out rants, whatever set him off. And though sometimes it was entertaining, mainly I wished I'd had a stun-gun handy. Then when life knocked him around a little more, he learned to control himself, and, where there had once been angry outbursts, there now came these protracted, sour silences. And I would make a point of testing the artillery, so to speak, to see if it would sputter out or like to explode. Sputter, usually . . .

"Very funny," he might grumble. "Maybe you should wear a special hat, you know, like for humor." Like a native New Yorker, he pronounced it *yumor.* "That's very yumorous," he might say, for instance, definitively. Watching him fail to rise to the bait or fail to dignify some exceeding stupidity of mine with a response, I would feel strange surges of affection for Aaron, because that's where I wanted our friendship to be, not quite at the end of something but near enough to the end so that speech was no better than an irritant. It wasn't like you knew what the other person was going to say, no, you owned it. The various personal revelations I turned a deaf ear to, of course. One day—this would be in New York now—I met up with him at the Zinc Bar (it was near the office), and was shocked to find him wearing a pair of very thick glasses. I didn't know what to say.

"I've only told you about a hundred times."

But it was news to me, this condition of his. I'd always thought...

"What d'you mean, a ploy? A *ploy*—?! Do you think I'm spending my days trying to think up how to win your sympathy? That's a hot one."

To make amends, I bought him a drink. To show he accepted my amends, Aaron ordered the priciest single malt at the well, took one sip and let it stand...

What he might have been—in a different world maybe, or with different talents—was a writer. He talked about the impossibility of it often enough. Once (again, New York) while he was out running an errand or trying to score drugs, I was satisfying idle curiosity in the drawers of his desk and ran across some of his work. I don't pretend my tastes are all that developed, but what I read truly embarrassed me. Lots of references to "torment" and "the abyss." It was pretty clear, in any case, the nature of Aaron's impossibility. I think this chance discovery—one not shared, of course—marked a turning point in our relationship, in an obvious way, and it clearly wasn't for the best. Now, whenever I heard Aaron go off on the subject of betrayal, I all but *resonated* with sympathy and understanding. No, it was no good at all.

New York—I never expected to end up here. It helped knowing Aaron had preceded me by a year. By the time I arrived, he'd been fired from his fact-checking job (he refused to share the details) and was working at the Strand, shelving books, where he stayed until he was legally blind.

My early years in the city are a blur now. I worked for men who were born assholes, career bullies, and, after work, I partied until I was insensate. Mostly clubbing, with Aaron, whose way I mostly paid. I learned to cope without sleep. There I had help, admittedly. It was like I was breaking, but breaking forward, into a new kind of conflict with myself. Others felt it too, I felt. I was more at ease with women, and I dressed up my act with what success told me was newfound grace. But success of a peculiar sort. I'd managed to push what I really wanted further out of reach. It was defeat masquerading as attack.

Aaron and I had perfected a rhythm together, which we played out—I want to say to the end, but that wouldn't be true. Things never fall together that neatly.

Or maybe it depresses me to think about how it did end, in a way. "'Let go.' Don't you mean *shit-canned*? Just what kind of lawyer did you think you were anyways?"

Not a good one—clearly. I had no passion to draw upon except for fear of failure and when I'd anesthetized that fear, there wasn't much in the way of competence to save me. But I don't beat myself up about it. Mistakes were made. And I don't blame Aaron either, although maybe I did a little at the time. My first few years out of the firm, making ends meet through a succession of grisly legal temp services and nonprofits, were a financial nightmare, but one which woke me from a period of intense and possibly permanent self-delusion, and for that I suppose I should be grateful, or so the therapist I'd started seeing then helped me to understand. It was also around this time that I met the woman who I willingly and without second thoughts would have married.

There were facets of Aaron nobody could deal with for long and not get irritated. The more settled I became, in my new job and with C—, the farther apart we drifted. I don't recall a scene or formal break, simply a growing perception on both our parts that the friendship was no longer tenable. He began to annoy me. Why had I allowed this guy to hold any influence over my life? I masked these feelings as best I could, but Aaron wasn't stupid, he could see I'd changed, and no doubt he too felt disappointment. Our communications grew shorter, duller, infrequent, then more or less discontinued.

Personally I would have preferred something definitive. In his absence, I tried to work myself up into fits of pique, remembering favors owed, money borrowed and never paid back, instances of extraordinary munificence on my part and great callousness on his, and I would prepare myself the way I used to prepare for trial, thinking up things he might say, then me coming back with a retort or sometimes a speech, and I'd go rigid with indignation. I'd even do this on the street.

I hadn't seen him in about a year when one day he stopped by the office for "a bit of free legal counsel," although he probably was hoping I'd offer more. I gave him a lot of unnecessary advice, tossed around some legalisms, tried to make the situation look as complicated as possible, all of it to prove that I was in my element. In short, I made an ass of myself. Aaron was having a hard time putting his sentences together, and threads of saliva would gather at the corner of his mouth. He used a lot of big words—correctly I'm assuming, but who the hell cared?—as if he, too, had something to prove. "See?" he seemed to be saying. "I may be a total fuck-up and I may be on my way to jail or out on the street, but I still have a healthy vocabulary."

Quite possibly, I asked him what drugs he was on, I mean it was that obvious. Quite possibly, I offered to give him a couple of numbers to call. Rehab, that sort of thing. Maybe he took serious offense and maybe, under similar circumstances, I would have, too. But the phrase hides a lot of things—second chances, third chances, half a lifetime of lifelines seen and not taken, and plenty of good old-fashioned fucking up.

Inexplicably, even though many more years would pass without our communicating, when C— left me, it was Aaron I thought to call first. I rang up directory assistance and after several false leads, located him in Astoria, at the top of the N line.

It was one of the first nice days of spring. The few trees planted on the sidewalk were tipped with green and the air itself seemed to be coming into leaf. The exhaust-blackened balance of the last big snowfall edged the curbs. I held Aaron's address, which I'd jotted down the night before on the back of another distressing bank statement. Our conversation hadn't gone too well, especially in the beginning. Aaron was phlegmatic. I got the sense that everything he said was some private sarcasm—*that* tone of voice.

"No," he replied to a suggested meeting place. "I don't get out much these days."

I was ready to give up. Why force a reconciliation? Clearly, he wanted nothing to do with me. Stupidly, though, I got onto the subject of C—, a dismal topic, and then came details I hadn't wanted to share, things that made me look like a fool or worse. Such as her last words to me right after she asked for the keys: "I was wondering . . . listen, would you mind very much walking the dog? I need to shower and I can't be late for work."

Aaron laughed so hard I had to hold the receiver away from my ear.

"Walk the dog!" he cried. "Are you the universal straight man or what?! Ha!! Walk the fucking dog! And what's even better, I bet you did!"

I assured him that he was wrong, but he seemed to be enjoying himself so much I didn't press the point. At any rate, something clicked, and we returned to our old footing, or close enough that Aaron invited me over.

"Keep your expectations low," he stated, "and you won't be disappointed."

Ironic that a dog should have been the source of our

reconciliation, for Aaron now had one of his own, a yellow lab with a very large head. Eva he called her, and their "bunker" was a basement apartment below a loud Italian family, its windows overlooking (at ankle-level), on one side, a driveway, and, on the other, a pathetically well-groomed but tiny plot of grass with a plastic, child-sized cast of the Virgin Mary. She kept her back to us.

He was now blind, of course. A placard hung from Eva's neck reading, IGNORE ME. I AM A WORKING GUIDE DOG. Those words ricocheted around in my head. They seemed such a surly and undignified thing for a dog— any dog, but this one in particular—to say.

He offered me a cup of tea: "It'll only take a couple of hours. Now that you're a free man, you have the time to spare." Taking invisible umbrage at this sally, I made no offer to help as he ran both hands through the eccentrically stocked kitchen cabinet, knocking over boxes of sweet cereal and cans of black beans and dog food until he found the Lipton's he was looking for, lifted out two tea bags, and then started to search for a pot, a kettle, anything in which water could be brought to a boil. Rice and pasta rained from their bags onto the counter. Aaron seemed to be injuring himself deliberately—releasing yelps of probably genuine pain—in order to prove to me how poorly he'd adapted to his affliction. I made sympathetic noises, but that was it. Finally, he grew tired of the game. "Tell you what," he said. "Why don't you just keep standing there?"

The place was a sty, no attempt to even kick the mess into piles. Plates scabbed with uneaten food, on his floor, on the table—and quite a few, along with assorted pots and pans, in the kitchen sink, which was also, judging by the pasty white streaks, where Aaron brushed his teeth. Sooner or later, you accepted the fact that walking around meant something breaking underfoot. The only thing not lying about—I was surprised, I confess—was dog shit.

The place smelled bad. Those filthy clothes, of course. But there was something more, or stronger, than the smell of mildew, sweat, fur, stale smoke and dirty feet, and while it was rank, I couldn't identify it, either as a peculiar amalgam of the smells just mentioned or as a separate smell, distinct but not yet attached to a source. It was the kind of smell you refrained from joking about. Too personal, I thought, but I was wrong. Rinsing out a cup in the sink, I noticed a saucepan in which the residue of a cheesy tuna casserole had been watered down and left for days, with a green gelatinous mold shaped like a sombrero on top. Backing away, I stepped on—and broke—a cheap pair of sunglasses.

You'd think I'd take the first opportunity to flee—hop a train back to Manhattan, clucking sadly to myself the whole way back. And for the first hour or so, escape *was* uppermost in my mind. After that hour passed, though, a surprising thing happened: not only did I feel obliged to stay, I wanted to. Is "want" the right word? Compelled, you see, by emotions which deviated from pity and by a new complexity bolstered to my old perception of Aaron. No, it was very simple. Blindness worked for him, and yes, I know how heartless that sounds, but there it was. It gave his existence definition, his failures *gravitas* and all his resentments worthy cause—this truly caustic resonance.

And I stayed. Afternoon stretched into night, and I switched the lights on, sat in that wrecked basement and listened to Aaron. Occasionally I said something. In most ways it was typical, ten different types of invective twisted into a spew so bleak and interminable it made your head hurt. In other ways it was like the doggerel I'd run across years earlier—laugh and its rotten spell was broken. His eyes no longer deceiving him as to the reactions he was constitutionally incapable of soliciting, he watched me watch him and listen to him, and, hard as it is to say why, I felt he had picked up a newfound dignity.

That night I dreamed I myself had gone blind.

But it was a strange, almost metaphysical blindness because, of course, dreams being a mainly visual medium, the capacity I lacked wasn't sight. Not strictly speaking. This dream was full of people and incidents of such totally bland character that they had to be spelling out "blindness," and among them Aaron stood out like a beacon. For some time after I woke, it seemed odd that everything in my bedroom was as I had left it. Odd, too, how it felt. I understood the message in my dream to be that seeing was nothing more than the habit of believing everything you saw.

Of course, part of my fascination included the dog—or rather the relationship that had developed between the two of them. He depended on her completely now, as he'd never had to depend before on another living creature, and he resented that. He must have. Resented the fact that she was always at the end of the leash, pulling him forward through the confused, noisy darkness. Resented her steadiness at sounds he himself would jump at. And most of all that she—a dumb creature—should possess the gift of sight. From what I saw, he treated Eva pretty badly, at times some truly ugly shit. I suppose I bear part of the blame because I didn't openly chastise Aaron. But what could I do? I feared this would only push him further when I was gone.

Instead I took the dog's side, silently but with vigor. Whenever I visited, I'd bring her a new squeaky toy, a chewable bone made out of brown vinyl or a can of doggy treats, supposedly good for the teeth. Particularly cruel, Aaron thought, was the time I brought over a little beanbag cat that yowled whenever you tossed it against something hard, on what turned out to be his fortieth birthday. That I hadn't known (or remembered) made no difference. My apologies were so much wasted breath. He rose to the occasion, with a great show of hurt feelings, a performance cruelly wasted—we both knew this —on the likes of me.

Because all I could think was that he was going to disturb his neighbors. I suggested we take a walk and offered to spring for dinner, any place within reason. The fresh air worked as a calmative of sorts. It was late summer and we walked north, following the channel. Other dogs would bark from behind fences, the sight of

Eva upsetting them. Aaron would jump, then start yelling, pointlessly.

I watched Eva stretch back her hind legs and quiver as she plopped three turds into the grass. Her ears flattened in a wonderful imitation of human embarrassment. She tried to backpaw dirt over the shit, only Aaron yanked her away.

"All right already—*leave* it!"

We were in a fairly sizable park a ten-minute walk from his miserable pad. Mostly grass and hardwood benches, where old men slumped, watching us without real interest. They weren't even carrying bread crumbs for the pigeons. There were a great number of diseased-looking birds around. I'd thought the park charming on my first visit, but that day it had a profoundly depressing effect on me. Also, it would be the last time I saw Aaron alive.

I missed it in the Metro section of the Wednesday *Times*. A snippet on the ten o'clock news caught my interest, even though I didn't know it was him I was hearing about—didn't make the connection. A subway accident. He had been led too close to the edge by his guide dog, fallen onto the tracks, and ... people looked on—helpless, horrified. Had he yelled any last words, anything quotable or true to character? Somehow I think he must have, although I have no idea what they were. His guide dog observes from the platform as the train bounds, screeching, into the station. Eva. That's right. Who I then agree to take.

No, I didn't agree to anything. I offered to, *insisted* on it. I was told there was a good possibility she'd be put to sleep, and it seemed at the time I had too much on my conscience to allow that to happen. Now I see that saving the dog worked only as a glum and even meaningless form of expiation. It was one of those traps I have a genius for making and then stepping into.

My apartment was small. I had gotten accustomed to being alone—nobody to worry after, feed, groom or walk. I was jealous of my privacy. Having a dog, I discovered, is not such a small commitment.

So at first the difficulties were all on my side. A period of adjustment was needed. I say "at first," because, later, after a couple of months, the problems seemed to have a lot to do with Eva, who had changed for the worse. Did it start with the barking? In one sense, yes—and how easy things would be if there were nothing else to it. I mean I *tried* not to view her as responsible. I tried to let the past settle, and with it, the question of her guilt. I tried not to endow a look—did she want to go out?

again?—with personality, planning, patience, but something got in the way.

As I said, a period of adjustment was required. It lasted four, maybe five months. Nothing much happened during that time—my routine was thrown off and I developed a new one, accommodating the animal that had killed my best friend. Now that he was dead I felt I had the right to think of him that way, as my best friend . . . now deceased.

I never did see the body, but I doubt it would have helped much. My thoughts of Aaron were too unreal. Trying to conjure him up, to fetch him back, I often found it was myself I was thinking of. I made a lousy reality filter, I realized. I missed the quality of his voice and couldn't find the clubfooted consonance of his Brooklyn accent, so even when a word or words seemed right ("toit," "detritus," "revenant"), the delivery never was. I didn't comfort myself with the thought that nobody else tried or even cared. I walked his murderer three times a day, four on weekends—usually west to the river. I sat around patting her head or scratching the backs of her ears, while she would tilt her neck back to take full advantage. I called her a good dog and asked her who was a sweet girl, and so on, as if I meant it.

Only once did she let her bad intentions show

openly: I was petting her in the lower stomach area, trying to locate the nerve that would make her hind legs quiver, when she made a sudden lunge for my hand. She could easily have taken off a finger if I hadn't snatched it away in time. We stared at each other then, both of us shocked by her boldness. There were strings of saliva dangling from her sideflaps, and—astonishingly, I think—I checked my own mouth for drool!

But the barking. The slightest noise, from the halls or in either of the apartments next to mine, would set her off. It was a loud bark, it went through you—or me—like a shot, and it carried. Neighbors complained, the landlord threatened. Sometimes I would have to smack her with a rolled-up magazine to get her to shut up, but that didn't happen too often, thank god. The point is, she was out of control, and the constant barking was driving me nuts, too. It affected my sleep. Sometimes it even carried into my dreams, as the sound of a hacking cough, for example, or a pile driver, or as someone pounding on a door. Only once did it register as what it was, but this time I was making the noise. I was down on all fours. I remember being wildly agitated, whipping myself from side to side in a furious, doglike frenzy, as Eva reared back above me.

I woke with my head in a vise. The dog of course barking like a crazy person and my neighbors hammering on the walls with their fists. I swallowed a couple of ibuprofen tablets and stayed awake until it was light out. And then I took her for her walk, the same routine as every other morning, only this one was colder—ridiculously bright and ridiculously cold. My breath left crystals on my scarf when it wasn't steaming up my glasses. Every time we hit a patch of ice, Eva would pull at the leash extra hard. Come on, I thought, we both know it'll take more than that, and I bent my knees and stayed lower to the ground, as if preparing to slalom.

THE MELTING GIANT

It seemed to tear the top half of his head off. The new Santa's laugh was that awful. Terrifying. A baritone but not *Ho Ho Ho* but a laugh that was also a cry for help. *Help me!* he laughed, and the children on his lap were reduced to tears or fits of screaming.

"Do yourself a favor," said the manager, as he cut the check.

"I know," Russell interrupted with a grimace. "I know what you're going to say."

"Bud, if you've heard it before. Jesus."

So seven years pass. Seven holiday seasons and not one rolls by but Russell Richards doesn't feel the pang. Temperatures go down, the trees go up with their tinsel, trinkets and blinking lights, and Russell starts to get angsty. *Do yourself a favor.* It's a voice inside him he can't turn off. Instead, *why should I?* he replies. It's his catechism. A never-neglected routine. But the little ones still take fright of him.

That seventh year started off on two left feet—first a foot of snow over Thanksgiving, but later that December, three days of late Indian Summer, days so apocryphal and mild they seemed to belong on the April calendar. The remaining leaves clenched into little brown fists that shook at the buses wheezing past. Nannies and new moms backed the plastic off their baby carriages, neighbors returned to stoops, old men to the windows out which they'd stared their summer enmity, and Russell was moved to join in.

He joined like one granted a reprieve.

The passengers on the F train were good at avoiding eye contact. There was sincerity in their avoidance. It wasn't easy for them because Russell was a scene unto himself. He seemed to be handing out licenses to stare.

He grabbed a window seat but couldn't help but spill over. Although people were standing, nobody contended for a share of the seat next to him. He peered out on avenues laden with the dust from truck traffic and a mix of warehouse blocks and blocks of three-to-four-story brownstones, with their raked roofs all but touching. The train elbowed west by northwest before heading underground.

They waited in the darkness of the tunnel for the dispatch signal. The other riders dreamed fitfully inside the car, in those empty minutes, in the intimate anonymity of the delay. Their impatience hatched side projects, the obligatory groans of *why me god, not again, motherfucker, why now* and *it don't end*, and the other insect racket embedded in their ears. Adjectives latticed across different faces: they appeared to him as on a sign. The signs ran the length of the car, all variations on the same theme. ESCAPE FROM EVERYDAY LIFE. Buy your bank tickets online. There was no way of escaping them. Look, don't look, they'd find a way to seep in, look out the window, bare bulbs illuminating graffiti tags on the crossed lattices of pillar and post. Things were scurrying off behind. It was rat heaven out there. All the rats killed above ground, rats from all over the world, ended up in these tunnels, enjoying the filth and darkness, the human world enunciated as noise and delicious offal.

Russell repeated his catechism and that particular slice of heaven held off for a while longer. After several false starts, the train roused itself and staggered on.

Slant, facing diagonal from him, near one of the sliding doors, a toddler in a stroller watched three grown-ups who were making faces, cooing and hedging behind their fingers. The two women were obviously related, an old lady and her rosy-cheeked, middle-aged daughter— the giggling man next to them, not—but which of them the boy belonged to, Russell couldn't guess. The antics of the grown-ups were so well choreographed the child might have been communicating telepathically. *Puff your cheeks out!* he'd command, and they would obey. They would huff and blow and pout and puff and their eyes would squint, like they were about to eat dirt sandwiches.

Then, without warning, the child turned his little extent in Russell's direction. There was a moment of indescribable intensity as he stared and Russell stared back. Russell felt weak with hesitancy, hope, nausea. He was sure the spell would be broken and the crying begin (with a phenomenal howl, if past experience was any judge) but this time things were different. The infant was stopped in his tracks, but surprise turned into puzzlement and he kept staring, not sure how to place Russell in his limited but growing repertoire of the uncanny.

Was this one a threat? The kid was, in his preverbal way, undecided.

And then he turned aside, to the two cornrowed men and woman moving purposefully down the aisle. Their hands were filled with flyers: she was handing them out while the men were sticking sheaves of ten or more into the bottom corners of the overhead signs. "You think you're messed up," the woman said as she handed Russell the slip of paper, but it wasn't clear if she was talking to herself or to him, asking or telling, rebuking or commiserating. It didn't matter. The child hadn't cried! *The child hadn't cried.* A victory of who knew what order of magnitude.

SEE THE WORLD THROUGH YOUR NEIGHBORS' EYES, he read. SEE YOURSELF! DON'T BE FOOLED BY APPEARANCES EVER AGAIN!

Remote viewing? But why not? It wasn't for the crazies anymore.

At 42nd Street, the people in the car poured onto the platform, out between two wedges of waiting passengers. Russell was a sizable impediment, but he was carried along, washed up one set of stairs and out the stiles and up another into the even warmer air outside. The humidity seemed to make the dust hover more than usual, filling in the thin winter light. The symmetry of Manhattan is the symmetry of a grid. You see it even in its name: m, nn, aaa, tt, h. It isn't a grid superimposed upon the clutter. The grid *is* the game. The stream of people divagated once they got above ground, and there were different currents, or causeways, to step into. Russell hesitated and so was jostled more than once.

"Watch it." An immoveable obstruction. "Lameass." A blockage. "Fuckinutjob." Snowbanks sank to the pavement, their runoff backed up above the drains at the corners. The salt thrown down to melt the ice was being carried down into the earth, beneath the trembling pavement and into the tunnels, corroding the cables wrapped snugly underground—like the city was melting back to life. The sidewalks couldn't fit all the people there were, and the impatient ones would shear off the curb, one eye over their shoulders.

The superstars of the WB empire were being dragged along the sides of buses. They lounged and bullshitted and laughed their way through the city, stopping every two blocks to let people on and off. His eyes traveled the length of these enormous reclining bodies. He walked slowly but couldn't help getting bumped from behind. It was very exhausting. Streams of shoppers, the working dead, tourists and their kids, the whole busy world. Sincere young women with petitions tried to waylay the ones who were trying hardest to avoid them. Russell's sister had been one of their ranks once, back before she'd given the world and him Max.

At present he came to a shelter from the streets, a corporate lunch-hour park slotted between the high sides and backed by a fountain, and he dropped into a wire-latticed chair with droopy armrests. Russell wiped his face with a damp sleeve. A young man sat down next to him, and of course it wasn't long before he started to stare.

Muzak turned softly from both sides of the building. *I was alive then,* thought Russell, *I knew that song before it became this booming elevator and side-of-the-building business.*

Clouds encroached upon the narrow wedge where the sky was, thirty-six stories above them. The kid was talking into a strange outdoor phone. "Sure, sure. I used to breathe through my mouth, too, you know. Want to know how I stopped? Yeah, well, I'll tell you anyway." He paused to listen. "Yeah. I don't care. Somebody showed me. Then they bribed me to follow their example. Whatever your objective, whatever the lesson, bribery is *always* the right tool." He paused to listen. "Of course it worked. Just what are you saying?" He paused to listen.

"No. Look, you deviant. I was yanking *your* chain." His eyes had a foxy edge and his cadences, if not exactly self-aware, lacked that *so-go-ahead-listen* indifference most urban loudmouths opted for. His carefully groomed stubble spoke more to his conceit than the suit did. The suit was expensive enough to appear anonymous. While he talked, he started paying more and more attention to Russell.

"I gotta go," he said, more than once, but the person on the line wasn't accepting that. It could have been anybody. Finally he clicked off and turned to Russell. "Do yourself a favor," the young man said.

"What did you just say?"

"I asked whether you could do us both a favor."

"Look. I'm not looking for unnecessary conversation."

"Okay," the young man permitted himself a twinkle of amusement, "but you certainly are dressed for it."

Russell Richards was perspiring heavily into his red suit padded out for the cold. Beads of sweat ran through his white hair and down through his combed-out beard and down his neck.

"Look," he said.

* * *

"What a coincidence!" the young man interrupted. "My name's Fenwick." He stuck out his hand and left it there for a while. Longer than most people would have bothered.

"Look. Whatever you want, I'm not interested."

"You're too uncomfortable for company, hey—cool. I just wanted to catch my breath. No rush, right?" He buttoned up his phone, which was still making noise—*talking* to him—and dropped it into a breast pocket. Then Fenwick leaned in with the air of one providing a confidence. "But ever since you stepped away from your responsibilities, my group's had to come to the rescue. Vital Vision Sectors. That's us! That's all I meant by what a coincidence! No harm done. So you can see why I'd be so excited, I mean beyond the normal reasons. Father motherfucking Christmas! All we're doing is filling in, of course. Just for the time being. Nobody's trying to replace you. What choice did we have? We felt it's our civic duty." He made it sound like *doody.* "You've walked the streets, but have you seen how it's really done? Earned the trust of the people? Did you make Christmas fun?

"Hell yeah you did! That's why I sit here in awe of you. I take one look and I see beyond those rags, to the glass of milk and the cookie, and I think, fuck. How the *fuck* did he—sorry, no offense, Father—do that? Inspire the level of trust so that you, a perfect stranger, could shoot down Johnny Nine-to-Five's chimney, into the family room, and leave these secret gifts—*gifts*, the word seems so strange, looking at you—from a total stranger from who knows where, underneath a tree, and then, while on your way out, back up the chimney, you take a little time out. What for? Why to fill up on milk and cookies. *Milk and cookies!* If we tried that shit—but we did. I mean *we tried!* And it was the cops when it wasn't multiple man ones. So, first of all, the first thing I wanted to do was to pass over some respect. Respect is due. And so forth. So. So—here we are."

It wasn't the speed of the spiel or the quality of insinuation that had Russell stupefied but the fight melted out of him. It was hard to say what it was exactly. His spirit, issuing as flopsweat, trickled to and ran down his trouser legs. Fenwick looked at the ground, overjoyed, and said, "to just think. *Think*—a puddle! The water in one of these city puddles holds dirt from how many shoes? How many do you think? Hundreds? Or thousands—?! Can you imagine the human petri dish that just *one* puddle represents? Did you ever want to get down on your knees, in the middle of the street, in front of one of these puddles, and look—and I mean *really* look—into it. But I suppose you step over your puddles, Old Nick."

"I do," said Russell, growing more and more miserable, "I mean I have. Millions of times."

"So what kind of rare coincidence is this? I mean I've got time on my hands as well. Why not unburden yourself. How did you decide to go around imitating a saint? No offense. I don't mean you're an imitation. Your belt is really something. What do you say? Haven't you ever wanted to spill your guts to a sympathetic stranger?"

Never, Russell was about to say, but all of a sudden, he found himself starting to confess—how he thought his sister had no business having a child so close to forty. "... and on her own, like that. I told her so. So what? Why would that make me love Max any less?"

"Of course. Why should it?"

"That she would think that."

"Now we're getting somewhere. Oh, don't clam up. I'm sorry I said that. We had a moment of trust there, didn't we? But I pushed. Tell me if I'm being too pushy but, hey, I've got a fantastic idea! How about my gift to you is you don't have to guess any longer. No more guess-work, no more uncertainty about was it her or you who was crazy or just plain wrong. Right? How about it? This is what I have to offer. Right now, right here, but totally at your own pace. Certainty. On a completely free trial basis. No strings, no cost."

"Just go away. In return for what?"

"Like I said, it's *free*. Where's your Christmas spirit, Nick?" While keeping up his confident chatter Fenwick was fiddling with the brass clasps on his valise. He un-snapped one but the other seemed to be stuck.

"I don't know," said Russell.

"So fine. What? What don't you know? I swear they make everything these days to break. Let's see, yep—China again. If it doesn't fall apart in a year or less, some-body's head is gonna be on the chopping block. Doesn't matter how much you're willing to spend. It's not about the money. Goddammit! Almost had it there. No, it's the powers-that-be not wanting us to form material attach-ments. When did everything get so zen? What don't you know? Ah. Got it." He opened the case by inches. He was suddenly cagey, trying to reach in and rummage around with his fingers. This, of course, had the effect of making Russell want to see more of what was inside.

He started to open up. "I mean," Russell said, "I loved the boy every bit as much as she did. I could have been a father to him, at least more than an uncle. He *idolized* me when he was three. Couldn't get enough. And Nancy was the one who was jealous. Of her own brother! We could have raised him together. We did. For the first five years we were a team. What—" Russell stopped when he witnessed the extent of the confusion in Fenwick's briefcase. Papers, index cards, badly gnawed-on pencils, gnawed-at apple cores and wreaths of dried-out flowers—he didn't know what kind, but they'd turned a crusty orange. A grade-school primer. A sticker that said MEAN PEOPLE SUCK. Banana bunches of keys. Old, gunked-up coins. Some had got stuck together. An eclectic mix of DVDs, some pirated versions of recent releases, some Criterion quality, some he'd never heard of, and some, judging by their titles, pornos. *The Wizard of Odd* was one. The cover had a jockey-sized Svengali knee-deep in the genius of his trade. A tornado tore out of the Arts & Leisure section of the *Times*. There were *Times* and *Posts* and *News* from cities all over the nation, the front pages anyway. Generally speaking, the headlines weren't good. It was the telescoping of a vast disorder.

"I'm no mind reader," said Fenwick, "but my bet's on

Max. Something tells me he was behind your falling out with your sister." This was Fenwick's first mistake. Or should Russell say "Fenwick"? Because Fenwick obviously wasn't his new companion's name. Unlike the guesses that had come before, this one was too good—spot-on but with an edge of gloating around it, subtle but there. Maybe not *the*, but here was a devil so far gone he could take his comfort only in the suffering of others. Whatever could be wrung from such encounters. Probing old wounds. He had more than a gift for it. He'd made it his calling card. He roamed the city in search of victims. The incompletes. The defenseless slobs. A psychic vampire. Somebody like Russell would be like a buxom virgin to him.

"I *know* you," said Russell, and tried to shift his chair around, away from the intruder, only it had been nailed into the concrete. "I see who you are."

"And you think that makes us even? You know me. Shit, get off your high horse."

"No."

"No. No what. What?"

"Go away."

"Of course. How can you believe in other people's good intentions when you no longer believe in yourself?" Fenwick pulled a pair of sunglasses out of the briefcase and held them out to Russell. They were star-shaped and the powder-blue rims had glitter on them. "Everything you saw in that case? That's my workload for just one week. *One* week. On the positive side, think about all the lives I get to touch. Kismet! Just try them on, will you? For eight seconds. A second out of your life. Eight seconds and I'll leave you in peace. I'm not prepared to give up on you just yet."

But somehow he didn't make it sound like a threat, or even a promise. He was very good at what he did, this Fenwick. Hadn't Russell always imagined the moment like this? When everything would change.

That's what *I* am, this character seemed to be implying.

A chance to set things right, for the second (or seven hundredth) time.

He'd taken up the costume at first for the extra money. That was all it was back then, just a costume. The resemblance, even in his fifties, had been striking, uncanny even. After his mom died, Russell and his half-sister had moved into the Lower Slope brownstone she'd bequeathed them along with a small inheritance. By cautious investment, pooling their resources and renting out the top floor, they were able to achieve the modest dream of their generation: early retirement. To never have to set foot in an office again. To celebrate, Russell started growing a beard. He'd always been impressed by the forked monstrosities of the nineteenth century prophets, but when his own appeared, it was not just as white as snow—but just as fluffy. He had a workshop in the basement where he did carpentry, small projects— stools, mock ducks, doll- and birdhouses—and she took up worthy causes, most to do with the environment.

Through one of these, she landed herself a boyfriend, briefly. David stuck around long enough to get her pregnant, but when she decided to have the boy, he skedaddled to the opposite coast. But amicably enough to make Russell suspicious. Russell, who'd always heard Nancy tell it like anybody who brought a child into the world in the shape it was in would be perpetrating some kind of monstrous crime, thought there was too much symmetry behind it all. He double-checked the joint account, but found no evidence of an "arrangement." But that wasn't surprising. Twelve years younger, but she possessed his stepfather's devious intellect.

It was a long pregnancy but a short labor, a C-section,

and another three days to regain her strength. Russell visited her and Max at the off-white maternity ward every day, but the family feeling didn't hit him then. It was when she brought him home from the hospital. It was the moment she carried the boy up the front steps and went through the door, into the brownstone. *Ours.* A threshold was crossed. He was so tiny, adorable, so helpless you couldn't help but love him like your own better self but unformed and still open to impression. When he wasn't colicky or hungry or scared, he was an angel. But he surprised them both by how much a little baby can run up the expenses. Russell tried the department-store gig in Max's third year, expecting it to prove impossible or a joke, but what he discovered instead— besides how much a top-notch Claus can earn—was his calling. "Of course," Fenwick interrupted. The knee to dandle them on had already been broken in. That was when it dawned on Russell. He understood why he'd been so lonely his whole life. He had been relating to the wrong kinds of people. It was kids he was meant for— the *children.*

But could Nancy just admit to being jealous, she could not. She had to criticize. Insinuate that *his* affections might be somehow warping to the boy. In summer, she would say, "Why can't you wear a shirt when you're handling him?" "Because it's hot!" he would yell back. "Well, you're getting your sweat all over him." That was just one example. Not wearing a shirt! Was he so disfigured he needed to keep his shirt on at all times? When Max got older, she would ask, "What have you been telling him?" "What?" "I don't want you talking to him about people being put in stocks." "Why?" "Because it's weird—and it's disturbing him." She implied that he was causing Max's nightmares. Or that the nightmares the boy was obviously having—Russell heard him screaming, totally hysterical, every night—were Russell's fault somehow.

She was getting Max so upset he started to believe these lies as well. It was a mounting campaign. And because Max was a child, everything came signposted far in advance, everything that at that age was sure to be fatal. Russell felt the distance between them growing. It was just a phase, he told himself, but it wasn't. It was his sister's neurotic moodswings that chipped away at her boy's love for him. In despair, he banished himself to the basement, for longer and longer periods of time. And then, after the last rebuff—so childishly insensitive Russell found himself incapable of not bearing a grudge—

suddenly everything was past the point of repair. "He's not *ours*!" he remembered Nancy shrieking at him, from that remote time, with impossible violence. "He's not *yours* to punish! God, Russell, do yourself a favor, and *get some help!*"

When they moved out, his own nightmares returned. He was in hell. He ate a potato chip, and it tasted like hell. It was like biting into paper. The salt burned into his tongue. The Juicy Juice he drank was all aftertaste, but it did nothing to slake this horrible thirst. His, he believed, was not a self-made hell but one imposed from the outside. Those who ensnared him, glib imitations like "Fenwick," they were put here to test him. His sister foremost. And for what? He could conceive of only one answer, and in the grief of his betrayal and his days and nights of lonely suffering, the answer quickly grew to possess him, into assuming the shape of a saint. He would show them both by *becoming* Father Christmas.

But the little ones all took fright of him.

He felt the burden of shame his costume was carrying from the rank sweat and picked up the glasses Fenwick had set down, and he put them on. The lenses fogged up immediately. The blur got bigger until it included all

Midtown, the whole city melting into facets of yellow and orange while his eyes watered with the effort to make sense of them. Tears of concentration ran down his cheeks. He'd all but given up—it couldn't have been more than five seconds—when the riddle resolved itself. He passed into focus and saw he was looking at himself. It was extremely disorienting, but he appeared (so it seemed) through his companion's eyes. *Now* "I" *am Fenwick.* But as soon as this thought popped into Russell's head it popped back out because only the eyes were affected. The other senses stayed his. They were keener, in fact. With sight deposed—"thrown over," in a sense—touch, taste, smell, and sound all fought for the priority spot. There was confusion in the scuffle, some mix-and-matching. The whisper of anise in Fenwick's voice, like he'd walked out of an Indian restaurant. Or himself, salivating through his skin, watching himself surrender, drip by drip, to this creature of intrusive and irrational empathy, back into the pavement, drop by drop, the salty sweat of one word dripping off his tongue. "Holy—"

"By all means," Fenwick said keenly. "*Look!* It's apt to change your life."

The ingenuity of his bluff was staggering. Russell

watched himself take the flyer out of his pocket and look down to reread the printed words on the consignment, but of course that was impossible. Fenwick put out a hand and Russell didn't hesitate, he passed along the slip of paper as one would a ticket to a nearby Broadway show, and through Fenwick's eyes he read—recomposing with barely a glance the impossible words, while watching the light which surpasseth understanding break, burrow down and dissolve into this intensification of painful enlightenment pictured in front of him—BEHOLD YOURSELF! "Remote viewing," he said. "Sure," said Fenwick, without batting an eyelid, "we're *all over* that." He tucked the ticket away in his briefcase. And at first it was like boric or hyperbolic acid, the vision burned his fragile idiom that bad. It seared the wonder in the flesh dissolving there in front of him, and it was his, all his. Fenwick wouldn't shut his eyes. Or was it all in innocent fun? Russell's only other choice was to take the shades off, but knowing it was that simple was the hook. But what was he looking out at, eyes filled with this odious but unarguably genuine empathy? The memory that worked on him and worked on him, to this day. The little pippin. The hypogriffin of seven years' disaster. In his candy-cane-colored outfit, he was making all kinds of surprising faces, trying to win back his child.

"Uncle Russ," Max had said, "you're silly."

"But of course I am," said Russell. "All grown-ups are fundamentally silly."

"But why?"

"Because," said Russell, "think about it. There are really only two ways to be an adult. Silly. And scary. It comes about through our genes." But wasn't there the man of sorrows as well? Mortal after all. He saw the face tackle his memory. Russell took off the shades and rubbed his eyes. He rubbed for a long time, reluctant to open them. When he did, Fenwick was gone, but the glasses were still in his hands. The sudden emptiness of the plaza, augmented by the many chairs casually arranged around the slablike tables, but, in fact, *riveted* in. At the back, a curtain of water fell stiffly down the front of a distressed metal tablet. Quick claques of pedestrians, tourists and suits, walked past on the sidewalk, but nobody turned in. In the break between sides, cars streamed and stopped. Local and entertainment news on the minute wrote itself across the red news tape banners, across wall-eyed windows opening onto snapped-together cubicles, with the different speaker systems disposed of—camouflaged—around the plaza.

The music deferred to the vacuousness of their physical attainments, while also secreting something familiar. Russell knew it. He had heard the original version thousands of times, but couldn't remember the name. Not the name, but for reasons impossible to fathom the lyrics did come back to him. The people were passing faster than the cars, as a rule, and there were more of them, and they seemed more diffident and fragmentary as a result. Clips of color, of material yearning. *For well you know that it's a fool* (he remembered) *who plays it cool by making his world a little colder.* And all the words returned, right up until the chorus.

Meanwhile, Fenwick's speeding south on Fifth, feeling pleased with himself. More than a little. What a stroke! Luck like that is like winter lightning—but what about his technique? He'd been very in the moment. Twice this guy had almost wriggled free, but he'd reeled the fish back onto the sidewalk. It's so rare to run into a presenting type that you imagine they've all but ceased to exist—the Napoleons, the Christs, the Lincolns, Washingtons, Kennedys and supporting presidents, the prophets, martyred saints and holiday enunciations. He, Fenwick, believes himself to be an original. His walk certainly is—ditto his *glide*, angling sideways with one shoulder, with the arms coddled loosely, not swinging back and forth too much. The pace is brisk but conveys no actual hurry. His wending is a private-in-company performance, but he devises his way between clients and potential customers—who are keeping reasonably clear of him—while also avoiding the man- and weather-made cracks in the sidewalk. In fact, he is making all kinds of minor metaphysical calculations as he passes different pairs of eyes, eyes connecting with his or not. He keeps pace with these early impressions, it's easy, the UES thoroughbreds on top of Gramercy winsomes, cracker pontoons, wasp-waisted naifs, Japanese jokers and the more durable European duos so undeniable in their eager fashion nativities, corkscrewed after or plaited arm in arm like the boroughs that collide— but more naively outwards. But they step into his path and on behind, quarreling sports with their peers, while beside him angry workers circle an enormous inflated rat, both claws extending palms-down, as if to be slapped. An intricate nest of buttoned-up white collars. But the intricacy lies in how they slowly circulate around one another, taradiddle, square-dance style, using oncomers as moving bales of hay. It fascinates! Between beheadings—a blur of rapidly vibrating thumbs —some kids swap Texas instruments. This man's face narrows to a knife-edge while the wings of the moustache work outward like a vise. The competitive beauty of an almond-eyed office assistant, her slick hair brown but suggesting red. The veteran collecting small bills behind the cardboard sign that keeps him and his companion in misery, a brute shepherd mix, hungry, scatters his blessings indiscriminately, whether others provide or not. But who's really at fault here? Is "society" standing in his way? Hardly. There's something pleasant to look at in everybody, Fenwick finds—he gets a tiny sexual charge from every last one of them. But he gives back even more. What a job! He puts his mouth to an ear and blows. A few temporarily disintegrate, but not Fenwick—nor upon him—who deftly skirts the supplicating cap. But then he nearly loses himself, just as the sunlight loses heed behind the office towers, siphoned across avenues, down rundown chasms, first between Orthodox Jews in dark winter jackets and then between a Con Ed crew wrestling with cones, bibs and orange helmets, decked-out ministers of old Broadway vaudeville beside shock-haired deliverers and middle-aged PAs, location men, a white rasta with primped yellow dreads, gaffers, presumptuous Latin teenagers, lumpen Isises warily noted by Hoboken bluebeards in suede trenchcoats gleaming with close-of-day moisture, a coffee-carrying woman hurrying forward in a business suit and black tights as the sunlight forks along the cross-streets of the low forties, a swaggering subaltern in pink pinstripe, executive wool skirts, a couple of leg-warmers, knitters, tall and short—the scarf reaches down to her waist—and all of them, all, every last one, is talking to him- or herself. They are fashionable, glitzy, greedy, and hairy, but they are sublime as well. They call up the voices of friends cut off from them forever but surviving in the ether that surrounds Manhattan. "Insha'Allah." "Gotcha, man. Gotcha." ". . . but that wasn't the *extraordinary* thing. The *extraordinary* thing . . ." Fenwick flips it around. And when he's done with the friction of minutely loving these people—loving them for who they appear to be, not are, for the typological questions they pose, with their wonderful suggestions of intricacy—he finds he has arrived at the preening lens of the times that is Times Square. Here the giants and saints of this world compete for Russell's attention—who, from his perch ten corners back, is peering through those discombobulating glasses. But now he is able to see as Fenwick sees them, as funny adjectives that hope just keeps stringing along. Circulating. So many but all communicating to themselves. But the thing is you didn't worry! Because the best cure for hope there is is laughter. It rolls up out of his belly and spills out of a pure spring tapped from the source, an enormous surcharge, out over the intersection—but actually *funny*. Santa's new laugh is terrific. Focused and infectious. People stop and smile at him, but it's a good smile. They are curious and engaged, all but prepared to fit themselves into his unkillable good cheer. As laughter goes, it's hearty but far from seeming deranged. It binges on that last shot of sunlight scraping down the aisles. It obeys the worn-out brightness of that moment, and the theatrical bills of Midtown. But here. Now.

BITTER ANGEL

1

I started seeing her. On a Wednesday, Ash Wednesday in fact. For a nonbeliever, the sight of all those foreheads smudged with crosses materializing and vanishing inside a crowd of well-heeled strangers brought a charge that was immodest, esoteric, serene. Not one: we are none of us as unique as we like to think.

2

She was bringing two beers from the counter back to our table when she knocked over a stool and spilled onto some woman's new leather jacket. And it became clear: her mood swings, the careful attention and broad hints from her best friend. It made perfect sense. I was all nerves and trepidation. That wasn't unusual either. At this stage, failing to make a pass would have counted as a silent but definitive no. I'd been toying with the idea, I said to her half an hour later, walking toward Market while she decided whether to invite me home for the night, or "hanging it out to dry."

Back at her place, we spoke piecemeal for a few hours before we began (tentatively) to unfold.

3

Six months earlier she had shown up at the crisis counseling office where I worked to begin her temporary assignment. I'd answered the door when she rang and informed her (nobody else around) she was a day ahead of schedule. She appeared nervous, as who wouldn't be on her first day of work. She did a rabbit-twitch with her nose and mouth, then left—or, to suit my fancy, vanished back into the hat. I noted four things about her then: that she was got up all in black, including the greased and dyed hair; she was breaking out; the lipstick, a damson shade thickly applied, seemed too much for her small, pursed mouth. Fourth, I noted her eyes, a chastening blue. Several days earlier, I'd spent the morning of my thirty-first birthday with my mom (visiting from back east) and grandmother at Pilgrim's Haven, in Palo Alto, where my grandmother, blind and bedridden by a stroke, spent the time conjuring what sense she could from the voices on the large television set in a metal bracket in the upper left-hand corner of her room, jumbling up the soaps, the sitcoms, the cop dramas, the cartoons, the game and talk shows, the movies of the week, and the commercials, and waiting for her daughters to call so that she could yell or plead for them to come take her home, as she hadn't been told the family house, designed by my grandfather in the 1920s, had been sold, torn down and replaced with a near-windowless monstrosity that, in accordance with the fashion around Stanford at the time, resembled nothing so much as a mausoleum. Pilgrim's Haven was comprised of flat-roofed, elongated bungalows, prefab-looking with a light metal coat of robin-blue over the siding, connected by open walkways along meager plantings of flowers. There were no trees anywhere. There were, however, several broad, boring lawns.

My birthday fell on the thirteenth. Given the reversal, thirty-one seemed to promise new beginnings or the auspicious overturning of old habits. Later at work I was given a chocolate cupcake with a single candle shoved into the top, and a hibiscus. I didn't really understand why they'd included the flower. I stayed home that night and watched TV or read, one or the other.

Brigid and I hit it off quickly, a rapport built on shared work assignments, common interests (music mainly), and of course the fact we both smoked. Before finding a post at the crisis center, I'd been transcribing worker's comp psych-evaluations at a mom-&-pop shop playing both sides of the fence. It hadn't lasted long. For one thing, I'd been optimistic about my typing speed, hoping it wouldn't matter. The near tapless slur of the two other receptionists' keyboards quickly disabused me of that fantasy. I also got the sense that something about my bathing habits bothered my employers, or the state of my laundry, the thrift-store jacket and birthday ties. Neither psychiatrist liked confrontation much, but they had their receptionists well trained.

4

"Why?" Brigid asked. "What is it you want out of this?" Her tiny hands fists in the pockets of a blue-and-green tweed jacket. I could have said I didn't have much to lose, and she had the most beautiful neck, a dancer's neck, but why? "I've examined the situation closely," I noted, "and found certain aspects to my liking." "Such as?" *Girls!* Ultimately she bought my act, or tolerated it. As sold on me as I was on her, but in her own way and with whatever scruples she supposedly possessed. Also she had a cat.

A semblance of carelessness coupled with the sense that, however silly what she said seemed, she'd laid down the law. On the phone she sounded younger, scarcely thirteen. "You don't even *try* not to be difficult," in a voice that was high, equable, reedy. She'd meant it (she hastened to add) as a compliment. The best people were all impossible, supposedly. Or "supposively": that's just how she said it.

Nob Hill Sunday: our first together, in a cupboard park at the top of the stairs of one of the city's premier hills, stretched out on a crowded lawn. I turned myself from back to stomach with the regularity of rotisseried meat. The park was tithed into uneven quads by radial paths bricked neatly through the grass. We'd stationed ourselves at a fairly isolated spot away from Grace Cathedral. She would tell stories, assuming I cared, no, I cared, not opening up exactly but telling me enough about her childhood to give me an idea of the role she wished to inhabit. A survivor ... we strayed into the topic of suicide, which she'd attempted (age thirteen) by swallowing a bottle of aspirin then going next door to play. She'd landed in therapy, which became an ongoing thing.

Obtained from eight years of treatment, as far as I could tell, was the ability to talk about her upbringing without embarrassment, self-pity or for that matter much emotion at all showing through. *Abuse* ... she skirted the word, and so would I.

5

As I said, chiefly as I saw it then. There was no edge to the conversation to drift back from, but we did move on to other matters, wherein she laid claim to telepathy, a guardian angel, the gift of second sight. My head rested on a black bag loaded with books. I shifted them a bit, bag and head, beneath leafage affording patchy relief from the surplus of light granted between fog and bay. It seemed a lull entered. We were learning how to become comfortable with one another, and silence (an easy one) was part of the process. I noticed something I had failed to after seven months of working together: she was extremely judgmental. People-watching with a view to picking apart fashion blunders was a favorite pastime. I joined her games with the savagery I often mistake for wit—she found me funny enough, in any case, if somewhat slow-witted ... "Can't you keep up?" she might say, but not in a mean way.

Later, I showed her the beginning of a story I was working on, written in the first person: a young man named Fellows goes into a pawn shop, where he discovers a large fossilized beetle, a scarab, and buys it without a second thought. Taking the subway home, he notices that all seven people in the car are wearing wigs, while only three of them are old. I told Brigid this had happened to me once. "On the BART?" she said in disbelief. "No, not here, in New York—it was the last car but in the afternoon." "Did you have a wig on?" she asked. "No—of course not." "Then not everybody in the car was wearing a wig," she said, pleased with herself.

I was to meet her at her apartment, after work, and she was late returning from ballet class. I waited at her building gate for half an hour, walked down to Market, came back to her foyer, waited some more. A pool hall on the second floor of the building opposite. Paddles of ceiling fans visible through the open windows, and a RACK 'EM sign flashing orange to green. I decided to wait another ten minutes, then leave. The time passed and as I walked down the street—approaching Market —I saw her at the far corner, and even though she saw me turn around and knew I had seen her, she began to run, not clumsily but endearingly off-kilter. She told me dancers were often clumsy. Sure, I watched her practice: she wasn't shy like that.

Features that (once they operated on me) were difficult to forget. She tapered sharply at her extremities. Taking her hand in mine, the fingers extended no further than the first joint of mine. Her feet were just as small, her head as well. The neck, her favorite item, long and set at a forward angle. Twice while we were together, she'd hacked her hair short in back. Just taken a wedge between her fingers and ridden the scissors through . . . the dreaded "bowl" haircut. It was becoming too glamorous, she'd inform me after the fact. Once she did it because she hated the haircut I got, clipped a half-inch from my scalp. She had a round face. Her aquiline nose started high and sloped steeply on each side to close-set eyes and her blondish lashes bolstered with mascara, a night's sleep making horror-film bruises out of the sockets. She bruised easily. Knees, shins, thighs. In photographs taken years earlier, in unhealthy pours of sunlight producing a squint, with beach-length hair, she looked older, wearing a self-critical expression that seemed to confirm the worst. Part of her attraction was the innocence chiding any effort to honor or appease it. To which she owed so much incredible experience I felt like the ingénue—no, I *was* the ingénue, we both agreed.

When she told me her breasts were "torpedo-shaped," I agreed. Pointy with wrinkled, red-brown aureoles around the nipples. They suited a figure brisker than slender, erotic in the androgynous fashion of the day. The year of the flapper had finally arrived.

6

Like in a cabaret, a fly had glued itself to her face. I was caught short by a sneezing fit, three in succession.

We repaired to the public restrooms in the Fairmont, she to pee and I to get toilet paper for my nose. The Ovaltinetoned lobby: carpeting, drapes, lifeless frippery, lounge seats and sofas in plasmal upholstery. She called it the hotel for rich white trash, where her grandparents, aunts and uncles on her mom's side stayed whenever they came through town. She seemed to know her way around.

She told me about her father's belief system, sketched out its laws and his personal enforcement techniques. It was pretty bad, from where I stood—but she said he loved her and had adopted her as his own daughter. He worked part-time out of the house, as a financial advisor. Up until twelve, she received regular whippings with a belt. "Buckle end?" "No, but he used all his strength. I'd have to take down my underpants because he thought that might serve as padding." "How many times?" Afterward, I cringed at the questions I asked. "*I* don't know. I think I blocked it out after three."

The infractions were trivial, she said, failing to sweep the yard, forgetting to clean her room. On several occasions he'd slapped her using the back of his hand. Off a chair once. And once in the bath so she knocked her head against the faucet. She showed me the small scar deviating out of that. She was thirteen when the marriage ended and her father went into therapy. A period of tremendous remorse for him. For her a frantic reassessment of everything and everything's implications—her rage and mistrust and the suicide attempt followed. I don't understand this, but she stayed with him after the marriage to her mom ended. When I asked why, she said she stuck around to keep an eye on her half-brother. "I thought he was with your mom most of the time." But this was all she wanted to give me, and for once I didn't press.

I followed her down a white hallway, its walls lined with mezzotint photos of the Fairmont pre and post the 1906 earthquake, past a faux-marble bust backlit inside a glassed-off cubby, down a wide flight of stairs. My face on the wall-length bathroom mirror looked sallow, unimpressive. We found an empty banquet room, and she went into it with no purpose but to flag her own presence in its white-rose glamour, while I remained at the door, waiting to be busted or maybe admiring her as she walked through the empty banquet room.

* * *

Dancing, she moved as she had been trained to move. Sometimes in class, she'd add minor embellishments of her own invention. Outside the studio, silliness came to the fore. I liked her arches, from her eyebrows plucked above the bridge of her nose (where otherwise they would have met) to the soles of her feet, whose toes she let me suck on. The big toe was the most fun. Years of dancing *en pointe* had caused it to swell to the proportions of a fat cartoon thumb banged with a hammer.

7

New landmarks. Her last name was no good, she said, it had to change, and I felt duty-bound to have a go. Whenever conversation came to a standstill, I'd toss out a couple and wait for her unfailing disapproval. Sometimes I'd show up at her apartment with a single word on my lips, her new name, and she'd look back at me, not comprehending until she caught on. "Better luck next time!" Clemente. Comstock. Leitner. Haab. Radley. Versanova. Quimby. Nodabendon. This last, of course, being the name of heaven or the star system that the heavens of old evolved into, according to her father. He belonged to a local congregation of *earth channelers* who had distilled the varieties of religious experience into a sort of science of belief. Currier. Fairview. Lessing. Greene. Of course, she had her own ideas on the subject, and the name she at last found (I could only admit) trumped my whole lousy list. It didn't sit so well next to the first name, but otherwise ... she decided to become "Ms. Landmark."

The fiend with two faces. Her silver belt buckle monogrammed with the letter F—I asked what it stood for. "Fiend," she said, sliding the belt from her pant loops and slipping down to underwear in preparation for bed. I should've guessed: "fiend" was her watchword, her favorite noun for herself. In greeting and farewell, or just as punctuation, her friends would flash the "fiend sign," raising an index and pinkie on one or both hands. Me, I felt awfully remote from such things. Brigid took things a step further by claiming to be a Satanist: she was consistently advocating on behalf of "the universal destruction of mankind."

Brigid's naughty secret. Her other hallmark being her double (*bipolar*, when returning from her therapist) nature: born a Gemini. One side or the other laid claim to "an old soul." Whose? It didn't show. This proved something of a paradox: selfish yet generous to a fault—

closed-off yet almost impossibly self-revealing—unforgiving yet with a long roster of hard-kept friendships—sexually experienced yet uncomfortable with the whole process, at least around me, and so on. I tried to imagine Brigid's therapist based on the advice she gave her, but it was hard. And Brigid would have been furious if she'd known what I was up to with my questions. Up the block from her apartment, at the corner, a porn theater whose marquee never changed. One of the posters behind the locked glass in the entry was for a movie called *Brigid's Naughty Secret*, which she tried to purchase on several occasions without success.

Between moons. Between one moon and another, there never could be a choice. One an angel disguised as fiend; the other, friend. One disguise as good as another. How could I care? Either way I knew how it would end.

Smog. Not long after we broke up, I discovered that this *universal destruction of mankind* thing came from the liner notes of a local band whose drummer she had a crush on. A brawny beanpole, he attacked his set with great flair, with his back to the audience. I remember listening to the tape she'd made for me, high, on a shitty portable deck. Since I hadn't damaged my hearing yet, it sounded pretty good. Reverb was a sort of possession back then. She liked them, The Sea and Cake, Madonna, Elliott Smith, and the Cramps more than me, My Bloody Valentine about the same, and The Bats, Nearly God and the Dirty Three less. I remember listening to *Daddy's Highway* a lot, and *The Doctor Came at Dawn* once we were apart, as well as the novel science fiction of *Julius Caesar*: "she said I could do it without protection," the singer-songwriter would keep arguing, "that's not a woman at all."

Starcrossed. She wanted to be her own star, solitary but capable of defining (to some infallible degree) the orbits of those around her. "Others are free to feel differently," she conceded. "Others," I said, "including me." Because of this, I would call her "a free spirit" later, yes, meanly. Prime mover would've been more accurate: originating but not involved. "I don't want to have an impact on your life. Maybe I'm not saying that right." I told her she wasn't. "But don't you see yourself at least partially— and I'm not saying fully—responsible for the neuroses you claim to deplore? Can't you see what a fantasy 'no impact' is?" I couldn't come out and say it, but I felt I had offered her the simplicity she said she wanted to introduce into her life—and that simplicity, perhaps flawed by definition, was *me*—and here she was, rejecting it. But of course it was more complicated than that. We were returning from a disappointing dance performance. In some pieces, the dancers were suspended from wires against a wall that frondlike patterns of orange, green and blue were projected onto. The music was New Age chant, and there was a twenty-minute slide show. A long walk back down Mission, deserted enough to allow me to piss into a lot through the diamond of a chain-link fence. I was arguing that *all* dance performances should be done in silence, but at some point lost sight of the fact that she was no longer refuting me. At Van Ness I stopped at a cash machine, where we were pestered by two drunk homeless men. Brigid took the opportunity to explain why she couldn't give them anything tonight. She had a bad habit of seeing what she could get away with, offering her guileless empathy as substitute for an empty purse. This time it didn't work. One of the men began to mimic her high voice, and when she took offense, he responded with some nasty insults. The kindest being, "Ooooh, the little princess." After that the evening was shot. Knowing her fairly well, I would recognize her humiliation in the stiffness of her gait. She was quiet during dinner and increasingly disagreeable. I watched her take down one barrier and put up another, and I waited for her to strike out, not as most people would with an angry outburst, but with some cold flash of artificial insight, about me, the substance of which she would keep secret for days. Recognizing the con didn't matter. "I'll let you know," she said, lying next to me later, "if I decide it's real and not something I'm mind-fucking myself about. Now *if you'll let me get some sleep . . .*"

Michael and the entity Michael. The next morning, we talked about her last or last *real* boyfriend, Mike, and the entity Michael, a bitter angel hovering over our planet of tears, according to the *earth channelers.* "Tall, dark, and oafish" was how she described the former: "what more could a girl want?" Even though he was a control freak, a sadist, *and* a retroactive greaser, she'd stayed with him for three years—longer than anybody else, or than she'd ever want to again, she said—because of the coincidence of names, or so she believed. Michael and the entity

Michael. It was something you could say over and over. He'd taught her things about herself and about sex, and where the two coincided, that she didn't want to remember, at least not with me.

8

The lightweight pounding of the California surf over the yellow sand, pulling in, pushed back, the rubbing of two not totally incompatible surfaces against one another. Basically it was the sunlight, the oddly paramount light all day. The sky rustling up a cloud only to throw it far out over the ocean. A smog-blue suit. Their neighborhood consisted of hobbity homes buried in mineral-green hills and low cypress canopies: cottages resembling driftwood, immaculate white bungalows and rowdier structures feistily painted. But, basically, something felt "off." The climate for one thing: like it had stalled thirty miles from tropical paradise. The smog and clammy belching of the ocean made the air sit heavy. As in much of Southern California, smoking became a joyless habit, pure need. Perdidas Lagoon was separated from the inland flats of Orange County—as paved-over and packed with strip malls and freeways and rivetingly ugly homes as any suburb I'd seen, and I thought myself an expert—by a chain of pockmarked hills. The corniche north led through a brief deserted stretch of cliff-top dunes, then ran into thickly posted traffic, signals, retail clutter. To convey small-town atmosphere, the council had provided for a "greeter" who wandered the central limits dispensing hippie homilies, daisies, and Cheetohs. The wrongness seemed to seep out from within. And the inhabitants ... bumpkins with the manners of gods.

While big enough, the sole bathroom in the bungalow lay smack between the kitchen and her parents' bedroom (since the divorce, a study) and separated from each by a flimsy sliding balsam door. Brigid had mentioned listening to both her parents' noisy farting while growing up. In fact, her mom's flatulence was a regular theme. But the total lack of privacy didn't register until we went down to visit. There was the kitchen counter where her father would spend hours chopping, dicing, and mixing for the evening meal. There were cupboards stocked with pastas, grains, and spices from Trader Joe's. And then, behind that nothing wall, was the toilet where the three of them did their business. I had a hard enough time pissing with her father audible at the cutting board, on the opposite side. The idea of pulling down my pants ... no, no, it couldn't be done. Narrow though it was, the kitchen was the hub of activity, and more inviting than the living room cramped with antiques and knickknacks. The tall shrubbery in the garden kept the sun off most windows, but it also blocked the breezes. Relatively cool, but also a bit stifling. Her room felt particularly stuffy—the few windows in it high and slim, and the sliding glass door typically locked.

At least ten months had passed since my two nights at her father's house before I decided to draw from memory a floor plan. There were a number of sliding doors in the place. The bedroom was two steps above the living room. Inside a stand-alone glass display case on the landing between rooms sat an intricately detailed model of an early-nineteenth-century clipper ship three feet in length, with raked masts. It wasn't a room that accommodated outsiders. The majority of the oil paintings and charcoal sketches on the walls were by her father's grandfather, Impressionism stiffening into Fauvism. Over time the pigments had darkened to a creosote-type finish, including on Brigid's favorite—the most cheerful of the lot—a cockatoo with paradisiacal plumage. Of course, I took note of the bookshelf, which contained the California legal codes in thick blue volumes, and an assortment of travel- and law-related nonfiction. Given its own place of pride on a slanted lectern was *Channels of the Earth*, a massive tome. Next to the bookshelf hung a pair of Balinese shadow puppets.

Part of what made the room feel so uninviting was the antique furniture. It looked too delicate to sit on. As an outsider myself, I had to wonder what Brigid felt her place to be in that room, what pride she could take from the family tradition which her father—the stepfather who'd adopted her, as I was sometimes in danger of forgetting—so lovingly detailed and preserved. Her biological father had died of alcohol poisoning in Baltimore years after her mom divorced him.

One of the first things I noticed was the name *Nodabendon* burnt into a piece of driftwood above the pi-shaped Japanese gate into their yard. I asked her more about her stepfather's beliefs, many of which she'd been forced to share or contemplate while growing up. She remembered very little of it, but that meant nothing, she was never good when it came to remembering things. Her enthusiasm on the subject was genuine: unforced, if a bit starry-eyed. What I already knew was that they'd shared the shower, on and off, until she was nine, and that her first vibrator came from him. She called herself a daddy's girl, and it was true. Throughout much of our five-month relationship, she was barely on speaking terms with her mom.

A short walk down the hill to a Safeway, an L-shaped annex, the back-bar the supermarket, and, on the side, three or four small shops, one of them a pizza parlor. Teens out front, caps turned back, skateboards flipped up. Across the four-lane coastal road, waist-high hedges effectively hid the ocean. The bushes and the streetlamps deflected any sense that one was up against—literally, feet from—a serious body of water. Crossing the road and wading through those low hedges, one felt the rush when a curtain was swept aside. The purple depths foamed up at spiny cliff tails. We could see for what seemed miles—watching the misdirected spotlights from helicopters swoop the erratic line of the washed-against land . . .

9

Back in the Tenderloin she pulled out a high-school yearbook, and I looked over her shoulder as she flipped pages. She pointed out guys she had dated, kissed or made out with, at least one (always an upperclassman) per page. At thirteen she lost her virginity—a one-night stand about which there was some confusion—to a boy who left for Mexico the next day. "He was Mexican?" "No—listen, can't you keep up? He was travelling there over summer break."

The following year she joined the cheerleading squad. That was one photo she tried unsuccessfully to skip past. The year of her first real coup, a three-month relationship with *the* senior on campus, who she clipped because he was "too boring." The eight or so jocks, water polo players, surfers who followed left scribbles in memory, the kind one might jot beneath their predictable faces: "dork," "reject," "sleazy." She quit cheerleading after four months.

Came a time of all-night partying—beer parties, pot, 'shrooms—... at one she burned the inside of her wrist with the lighted end of a cigarette. A dare. I see you, see? You first. Something of that ilk.

In tenth grade the best friend of her boyfriend of two weeks committed suicide. The circumstances were bizarre: he'd been fighting with his dad and stormed out of the house. Later, when he returned, he found the old man dead. But what the neighbors discovered days after were two bodies, the boy's stiff between the toilet and the tub. And no note. In the winter of 1991 she fell for a skater punk who'd have sex only in his closet. It was hard not to get confused by her tales. She had a habit of coming flat-out with the most telling details, leaving the rest for rough imagining. When pressed further, her memory would dry up. She did tell me that if she were to have any regrets, it would have to be him, Eric, if only because things ended on a sour note. The details deserted her. She knew I was writing all this down. It had to be an experiment. Up until then she'd had trouble keeping the novelty intact, and when the "rose-colored glasses" came off, the flaws stood out. A sentence she'd read past. Love, like all sentences, has its period: hence our little experiment. But she began to worry about getting a reputation. It would start with the other girls— she was sensitive to the way they checked each other out, following her own habits, the rapid surveys and the unpitying mental calculations that took place all around them—and filter through to the male population, where the term "slut" had its own categorical charge. Mike was next. He'd trained her to experiment with him for three years. After they split up, he'd been taken in hand by a woman fifteen years his senior ("sort of like you," said Brigid), though he called her from time to time, claiming he still loved her ... Brigid and only Brigid.

"Earthquake weather." "Yes?" I knew what she meant, had read her mind: I thought I could do that then.

10

The apartment beneath us suddenly filled with rowdy partiers—music and thuds making the floor shake.

"Well," she asked, "what do you think?" "What do I think? It's your building. I think you should go down and tell them to shut up," I said. Instead, we went to see a Japanese movie about a guy whose face gets burned off, and how he goes crazy when he's given a new one. "I hate science fiction that turns the future into an allegory of the present," I said walking back from the Castro. Maybe that's not fair—maybe all sci-fi's like that. What it meant in the movie, at any rate, was everybody explaining what every stupid thing meant. When the man-with-the-new-face picked up a knife, you knew who he was going to stab and when. Introduce a brother and sister and . . . after they'd fucked near the end, she drowned herself in the ocean while he watched and was zapped into a Francis Bacon meat-monstrosity. "Why do you drag me to these things and then try to pull me out halfway through?" Brigid complained when I met her outside. She had a cigarette going. I took it out of her mouth, took a drag, and handed it back.

When I was her age and living in New York after college, I was called to my father's side while he struggled to survive leukemia complicated by Von Willebrand disease. A bout of early chemo pleurisy had landed him in the hospital, originally. I say struggled, and he did, but the incursions he suffered moved slower than that. When they'd tortured him all they could at B— Memorial, he was transferred to Rochester, where our family gathered in the waiting area with other sad cases, and where I read . . . *The Bonfire of the Vanities*, in a day, and *The Loved One*, shy of two hours. Although I disliked both books, I felt gratitude for the curtain they dropped and how radically they prevailed against the vision of my father lying in the ICU ward down the hall, connected to the IV bags that took four hours to deflate, fluid draining into his puffy arm. The gift of other lives, borrowed without responsibility. Weak as their blood was, it was enough. I read on a windowsill overlooking the front of the hospital, a grassy esplanade fanned to a sycamore- and elm-fringed street. Residential gabled homes three stories tall, comfortably subdivided. The weather was unseasonably hot for April. Under stewed grey clouds, breezeless harbingers of our future's endless summers, the new green of spring seemed like a horrible mistake.

Memories diluted by nothing but time, but I was nine years away from them then. Within that period, I shifted between cities—New York, Boston, Palo Alto, San Francisco, Los Angeles, San Francisco again, Boston again, New York again, Denver, Washington D.C., San Francisco again, Oakland—and in and out of the country.

11

"You kiss differently from how I expected," she remarked the first time she interrupted. Different . . . how?

With no further elaboration, it was reasonable to assume different meant worse. She was surprised I kept my eyes open as we kissed. "Well it's okay with me but what are you looking at?" "How about ... do you really want a list?" "No, but I'm curious." It was hard to explain because a face pushed that close was more like a flood, features washed serenely out of focus. Maybe I would look at an ear ... ?

The way she'd pester a necking session to pointless standstill. Her tongue was as dry as a cat's. We "fell upon" each other just once, and that came after a long evening of dinner and barhopping in North Beach with a couple of coworkers. Strained to the tearing point early. The looks we exchanged grew coarser. Our relationship was and would remain a secret at work. Locked into our roles and hating it, but loving the sight of the other locked into that role and clearly hating it. She slipped away first—a "shortcut" back to the Tenderloin before we hit Market. My excuse was more long-winded, less plausible. I proceeded after her, pulling up the collar of my trenchcoat and burying the lower half of my face in a scarf. Market's regular flood of crazies. Ugly neon shone through rolled-down gratings. After Powell Street, everything turned to shit—the tourist atmosphere near Mervyn's and the cable car plaza losing out to subretail squalor, stereo shops, trinket stores and strip joints, the Warfield and $5 barber shops with candy-striped poles, delis and smoke shops, the only places open at that hour. I stopped in one to buy a fresh pack. Between sessions, we'd snack on cigarettes and exchange words, only nice things then, and I would light both at the same time, like in *Now, Voyager*, while a green tram trundled past, sparks flushed from the power line on top.

The light sweat was mainly a function of the bulky down comforter, making her skin slick—soft, unquestionably—like an English bath cube once the water had seeped in. But she was strong and would sometimes press me to her body with such force I'd worry about cracking a rib. Her coltish quakes would wake me, suddenly, like she'd slipped one of her nightmares into my own thoughtless sleep, which I always would have a hard time returning to.

12

Over Labor Day weekend—two months after Brigid decided to simplify our relationship to "just friends," and several weeks after our last civil conversation, by phone—I hopped a bus for Reno to see my brother. He was there for a Housing Authority case, taking depositions. I'd vacillated, even though I knew I needed the time away. On Thursday night, two young women had knocked on my door and asked to use the phone. They were dressed like prostitutes, in high pumps, low-cut tops, and tight miniskirts, bangled earrings and jewelry. The plumper of the two, hair cocked in a tight cone with bangs dry as scissored paper, did the talking. It was pretty clear she was on something and in that state wouldn't take no for an answer. Reluctantly I let her in—reluctant because I hadn't cleaned the place in two months. We located the phone by its cord, pulling it from a collapsed tent of weeks-old weeklies, and she rang up her mother. Her boyfriend was in jail for purse-snatching or beating up an old lady, probably both, and she didn't have the cash to bail him out. She began to cry while insisting that she'd been clean for three days now—from where I sat, a transparent lie. She was cross-legged on my floor, talking. She cried. She circled back to the beginning and sorted through the details, some of which she'd overlooked while some she simply repeated. The next day I picked up a bus at the Caltrans station on Mission and First. "Silver Liner" read the ticket, but the bus itself was painted white with sloppy red stars and no name on the side. It was a day-excursion fare intended for eight-hour gamblers, mostly elderly Chinese women and a handful of decrepit widowers, and it came with a receipt for $10 in quarters at Harrah's, which I'd use later for laundry. Traffic was congested, stop-and-start until at least twenty miles past Livermore. Even beyond that there were bottlenecks, long stretches with little or no movement, cars stalled in every lane, most windows rolled up and reflecting through a fine scrim of orange dust, other cars and the bleached-out landscape of culverts and dry chaparral. The over-bright exposure made the faces of passengers behind the glass visible, but only just. I was in a seat behind an older gentleman wearing an oil-stained cowboy hat that stayed on the whole trip. Not that I cared. It wasn't like we were in a theater.

I would drift off into sleep so impersonal it seemed someone else's, then come awake and look out the tinted glass: simply noticing the outlets dragging past. Past Pleasanton, crossing into the Central Valley, the bus reached a regular speed, and I went out again, or back, as we crossed a cantilevered bridge over a river running its course between wide shoulders of chewed-up sandstone. I tried not to think of her, but it wasn't worth the effort. The book I'd brought with me, Fitzgerald's *Tender Is the Night*, lay bent back at the bottom of my bag. It was the 1934 version, beginning "On the pleasant shore of the French Riviera," which his editor would later alter by moving book two, the story of Dick Diver's first encounter with Nicole, to the opening. Years earlier I had read this amended version, with the chronology "put right," and while the differences between versions were large, I couldn't make an easy judgment as to whether it was an improvement on or (the standard opinion) a vandalizing of the original. Did it really matter how time traveled? In photos they looked like dwarves—their maniacally coiffed heads somehow too large for the bodies that couldn't be seen. Profiles chiseled in white chocolate. Dick and Zelda, Scott and Nicole. The resemblances unnerved me. The way, for instance, the word "lesion" kept cropping up: "again and again these branches went through the car." East of Sacramento, the driver pulled in for a rest stop at one of those plazas that attach themselves every half hour to the side of the highway. We piled out into blast-furnace heat—pressed on us from above, floating up from the black tar—which made everything unreal, people yards away fissioning into sulky gases. I bought a mango drink at a filling station and drank part of it. By the time we climbed back in, the juice was as warm as my own sticky, sweet saliva.

13

And disbelief. God, anything else would do.

OTHERWISE

BOX WITH STORIES INSIDE

Doug and Mary Monadoon had a pretty fair idea of what they'd gotten themselves into by the time they were handed the keys to apartment 440, in the exclusive Tollhouse townhouse with views of the Park. They'd learned the eccentric co-op rules by heart for the board hearing, followed by spates of interviews, and swallowed their share of bad coffee in the process, laughing to each other afterward. It helped that Doug was an excellent mimic. And his confidence (unlike Mary's) couldn't be dented. He knew his references were impeccable. Did that make the whole thing a referendum on *her*? Somehow Mary couldn't help but wonder.

A world on automatic, everything about the new apartment ready-to-hand, *in* hand already, down to the smallest detail... especially the little things. Schick blade and candy-striped foam whenever Doug needed a shave. Crushed ice from the alcove in her fridge when Mary wanted a cold drink. The big blue *Joy of Cooking*. Tea in delicate Lipton's bags. Even the potato chips came stacked. It was all so novel. Anticipating every impulse while remaining cunningly hidden from view was quite a feat. The apartment radiated "old-world" charm, even as it provided all the conveniences of the new. Worn in spots? Hard to light some of the odder recesses? A secretion of dust on inlays and molding? But all this gave number 440 its special character—the claim to antiquity Doug and Mary had been secretly wishing for, without knowing that was the wish, following the interrupted honeymoon. *A place of our own* was how they defined it, dared describe it aloud—inscribing their hopes on the noble city air. He ran through the morning classifieds, circling candidates in red, while she arranged things with the realtors. They'd meet at the Burger Heaven on 84th and "Mad," to do their hunting in the early morning or late afternoon. It was a favorite pitstop, for late breakfast or an early supper, and the underlined proclamation on every page of the menu, *No Substitutions*, never failed to crack them up. After each showing, they'd compare notes on how the sunlight angled through windows and onto the balcony, wood, or parquet floors ... variations in the inhabitation of its glow. Central Park was a wonderland from these heights —an unopened gift. It all seemed so novel to the pair of them. They'd decided to hold off on the lovemaking until formally settled into their first home together, and even *that*—in and of itself—was no reason to rush. In the Heaven, they made a point of passing items—french fries, pickles—onto each other's plates. Afterward, it became a catchphrase, a private one, which could mean almost anything. No substitutions. Doug bought Mary an enormous frosted cookie from the Big Green Baker next door, and then bothered her for a bite—"a little taste!"— all the way to her abode. She refused. "You bought it for me," she repeated—the logic was all on her side. They had so much fun just looking. Their energy and curiosity seemed boundless—yet the minute they began to flag, the Monadoons found the place they were meant to have. Doug went over the co-op rules with Mary every night, the week before their interview—"just for laughs," he said. He said this, Mary knew, so she wouldn't get nervous or flustered under the board's grilling. The apartment—number 440 on a corner facing southeast, a cheerful morning apartment—was so perfect she didn't want to blow it. The approval process was her only real "warning signal." Some of the questions on the form confused her. The nature of some of the proofs demanded seemed so—she knew the word couldn't be "inappropriate," yet she returned to it time and again. "I'm not sure how to answer that," she'd say to Doug, who—glancing to where she was pointing—replied, "make it up! Nobody cares!" "Suppose they find out?" "Find out what, darling? If you don't know yourself, how can there be anything to find out?" His logic was irrefutable—and, in person, the board was so much less intimidating than expected. The Cabots, a few years older than the Monadoons—an excitable, moon-faced couple who could have been siblings. A "prince from Corona" with an immense nose, inquisitive hazel eyes, and immaculate white gloves given to tracing delicate arabesques in support of his questions—in fact, they were closer to meandering autobiographical anecdotes. A slender man, he was approaching middle age. The two elderly sisters who lived in the fourteenth-floor suite directly above them, who repeatedly stressed the point that no two apartments in the Tollhouse were the same, as if that was important. In fact, very few questions were asked. It seemed all the board wanted was their attention and polite concurrence. "Did you notice, Mary?" Doug asked her later, "they all gave their apartment numbers when introducing themselves." "Did they? I was too nervous!" "Yes! Seems a good sign, don't you think?" "Yes! Like they were inviting us over already." "Precisely!" It was simply a matter of seeing things as they were—the temporary drapes slid apart—another fine day overlooking the boxed-in canyon of Central Park, its green tapping into the golden veins of fall. Colors of joy—and a faint, decadent melancholy—unrestrained. Yes, she knew it! The building had the whole *city* trained to respond to her and Doug's needs. Her thoughts went to him, and there he was. "Told you it would be worth the trouble," he said, coming from behind to wrap his arms around her—and squeeze. "But you didn't believe me." "Oh I do love you," said Mary. "Are you getting sick of me saying it—?" She attempted to unclasp his steepled fingers. His hands were like small furnaces. "Never mind, darling," he said, his words tickling her ears. "Do you think I need to shave?" He rubbed his chin. "You're crazy!" she yelled and slapped his shoulder—he slapped back, jesting but so carried away her cheek stayed red a full hour. Of course, Doug didn't work—the "career paths" open to somebody like him were all so ugly and sad, they agreed—but that didn't mean he remained idle. Rising early, he spent the daylight hours studying maps of Central Park and walking its perimeter, plotting optimal entrances and routes to ensure a safe and scenic first trip—an afternoon stroll, they'd decided. That night he brought home tulips and white roses from the florist on 59th Street—Howard's—and while Mary felt there was nothing to make amends for, she loved the gesture—and, of course, the flowers. They had a lovely dinner at home—Mary had supervised the pot roast—and then went two doors down for the Sinclairs' standing game of Hearts every Tuesday and Thursday. The Cabots had introduced them to the other couples on the floor, most their age—Doug took to Tom and Marty Sinclair especially. Tonight he shot the moon three times, while playing five others, and returned home slightly drunk and very pleased with himself. Mary began to undo his necktie—his shirt. The result was immediate. But why? What was the matter with her? "Listen," he said. "I have an idea. We wait until we brave the park—that'll make it even *more* special!" Mary felt it would be special enough now, but decided to agree. They necked a few minutes, and he fixed them each a cocktail. Was he trying to set the mood? What about when he said, "There ought to be a manual on how to do all of this"? He made a face as he sipped his martini, and then clarified—"You know, married life, parenthood, life on the *outside*." "There are!" Mary said, "thousands!" "Then there ought to be a guide to all the manuals." "There's nothing to be frightened of, Doug—just let go and let life take its course. Jeez, listen to me! I'm even *sounding* like you." "I know but I—I just want you to be happy." He popped two eroding tablets, downed the drink and rolled his neck around three times—quasar ablutions—and offered her a pair. He was clumsy and afraid—a fear he overcame or injected into her—rather selfishly, she thought, as if for the first time, as if remembering all the times she'd almost thought it. By next morning, it had begun: Mary vomiting into the toilet. She hadn't eaten yet, fortunately. "Which reminds me," she said, from her knees. "What's that—?" Doug said, not hearing her. "Where *are* all the children in the building?"

Days were for travel and investigation—nights research and cataloging. Doug wouldn't let her see the drafts of his plans. It was too soon, he said, and it was meant to be a surprise. He'd become so enthusiastic about the whole venture Mary didn't want to disappoint him. Everything had to be perfect down to the smallest detail. Columbus Circle was the obvious point of entry, so obvious most people wouldn't give it a second glance. But that kind of elitist thinking didn't wash with Doug. He checked it out—wandered among the tourist groups lumped about the outer plaza, likening its "grand boulevard" to a sunbeam stepping into fall's brazen arcade. There was charm to the spot, no doubt, but the throngs and smells—monoxidated horse and hay—couldn't be laughed off. More to the point, the pleading angels on the *Maine* monument's pedestal seemed too earnest a sign not to heed. At the southeast corner, a robot man who'd only activate for money. A quarter might sketch a shrug or brief hand gesture—a dollar issued full-body compliance, and more actual motion-potion routines, his expressionless face painted with some sort of steel-hued tapioca. Doug marched up and down Central Park West, from the cliffs sectioned by the 65th transverse to the shady garden at 72nd, peering through gates and gaps in the arcade wall—scoping Sheep Meadow with binoculars. The powerful lenses brought the people forward—readers, strollers, lollers, peddlers, picnickers—

so abruptly Doug felt he could seize the hairs on their arms, if he wished. There was something wonderfully contented about their attitudes. Some were couples, but most of them individuals who seemed to be talking to the air. He learned what he could about the landmarks. Shakespeare Garden, Belvedere Castle, the funny-looking obelisk. He liked the idea of the Ramble best, brisk knuckles with generous tree coverage, and a lake in a brush-hidden grotto. Whatever they did had to end there, begin and end, for it was his ideal. Like the other parts of the Park's midsections, it frustrated his best attempts to learn more—making it more attractive, truly *terra incognita*. He'd spot or learn about something on Fifth Avenue he'd want to investigate from the west (travel times around ran longest between 72nd and 96th), and he'd yearn—literally *ache*—with respect to access. Even thoroughfare rights. A feverish "gateway despair." How hard the reservoir proved! He'd seen it many times from up high, but it was impossible on Fifth—*any* view of the Park blocked by a steep embankment. West its bill could be glimpsed at the 90th approach, barely. Exploring access points on the east side, Doug encountered a gentleman in a sandwich board reading "Roper's Removal" on top, "Services & Extra" on the bottom with (reduced to outline) a hand holding a key circled in the middle. The placard behind was the same deal, more or less, but had "Roper's Removal Services" with no extras indicated. Doug was pretty sure this guy had started to follow him. "The thing is," he said, "it was the *sandwich board* that kept cropping up at different places—I can't be sure about the person." "What do you mean?" "You know I couldn't point him out to you. I'm reasonably sure it was a man, but beyond that— . . . well, he could have been black, for all I noticed." "Bizarre." "Yes!" Doug agreed. "I wish I could explain it." It was this very conversation that started Mary wondering whether, when she was talking to Doug, or he to her, or at least most of the time, they were talking about two different things, and what that might bode for any possible future they might have together, or happiness. Certainly his explorations introduced a care into Doug's ordinarily well-ordered life. Did it gnaw at him—? She touched his shoulder, and he grew tense all of a sudden, as though contact was incurable poison to him. "It seems like you're making a big deal about nothing," said Carter Tinkelpaugh, at a Cabot "dusk-to-midnight soiree" Doug swore he'd never frequent again. Callously, or at least taking callow pleasure in bringing Doug up short. "The parks have been safe for years now! Ever since our mayor started packing the criminal classes upstate." Before Doug had the chance to interject, somebody said "the sexiest man on the planet," and everybody laughed, and then somebody else commented on how quickly the suburbs had "devolved" into brutalizing endeavors. Mary found herself disturbed by the tone and terminology, which she noted to Doug later while trying to boost his spirits. "I knew you could have socked it to him—but I was so glad you didn't!" "Yes, I could have made a fool of him. Then I thought why bother? Guys like him don't learn, it's not in their DNA." And when he kissed her for the first time in what felt like forever, he stuck his tongue in her mouth, and for once her mutual dedication didn't surprise or send him fleet away, and they went on—jaws toothlessly chewing tongues, vertically sandwiched—for five minutes at least, until she felt she was about to faint. She went to bed to dream of the sheep she'd missed counting other nights, and woke refreshed—more than she'd been in a long time ... the seasickness of the day easing along with her sense of outrage. So what if the suburbs were contaminating their unlucky inhabitants—were they *her* poor?

In one, a down-on-his-luck businessman comes to the realization that a longtime acquaintance is drawn to men who are doomed, her honing sense infallible ... so when she shows up to rescue *him* at his seedy rooming house, in terror and denial he flees. In another, a soldier returning to his farm on a weeklong furlough buys his children a couple of rabbits, and when they are poisoned, he roughly accuses the day laborer. It turns out the deaths were his wife's fault, a stupid accident, and he returns to the war chastened by his rush to judgment. This story includes a vivid description of a summer storm, bringing with it "the illusion of a country divided evenly between the lights of catastrophe and repose." After a number of attempts (all failures), a horny bachelor figures out how he can seduce the new wife of an acquaintance—a redhead who wants men to be drawn to her ravishing intellect. The story takes place on an island. A mean drunk works magic on his neighbor of six months, molding him into a meaner and drunker version of himself. Going their separate ways, the two men ruin their lives and those of their families, relocating from one hilly suburb to another with the help of a red moving van. This story takes place not in Shady Hills, but the town of B—. On a whim a man swims from backyard pool to backyard pool—the length of a county—to get home, the pools getting clammy, the neighbors less friendly, the summer weather stormy and chill, time skipping beats as the swimmer dives into a shallow end, completes a lap and emerges dripping and tired, while the years pass, and he returns home to find himself locked out, alone, old, his wife dead, the house abandoned. Empty or taken-over houses feature prominently in the one about the unemployed parablendeur who burglarizes his wealthy neighbors. In one, the Monadoons discover their radio is able to pick up the conversations of other families living in the building—a source of innocent amusement, at first. One starts with an airplane drawn down by bad weather landing in a cornfield. One ends with a man picking himself up from the mud he's pressed his face into at "gunpoint," finding his hat, and walking home. In one, an improbably perfect family. One a "miscellany" of evasions. In yet another, the author spoke to Mary herself, attempting to impinge on her sympathies ... it ends suddenly when she snatches

the baby from her chattering nanny and is chased hel-
ter-skelter into the Ramble.

Increasingly, nights became about two things: Bridge
and Hearts. Doug and Mary enjoyed their submersion in
the Tollhouse denizens' uninhibited gossip, the opinions everybody wore on their sleeves, knowing they
were among friends. Lately, however, these parties had
been prompting friction between them ... both before
and after. Mostly it was Mary's fault. Without realizing,
she would say something to convince Doug that Tom
and Marty were about to "drop them," and he just could-
n't let it go. "I was only speaking for myself!" Mary said.
"But if *you* feel it's 'too much,' why shouldn't *they*?" "I
don't know," Mary said, "and I'm not about to guess. All
I did was express my opinion." "Yes—and you had every
right to! I've been very silly. We should start making ourselves scarce." "But we have to go tonight!" Mary said,
and Doug assented, back to his normal unflappable self.
At the Sinclairs', they were discussing the latest Broadway scandal. The turnover always seemed timed for the
Sunday spreads. The composer whose new musical,

Hannah Williams, had been breaking hearts over town. "Philip Tandy? He's hardly a lothario. He's quite tiny and stout. Has a white moustache. The whole Napoleon complex. Wears a beret." "*Always* wears a beret." "Yes, I stand corrected." "But he's got a terrible reputation," said a woman and the dapper young cadet-type next to her said, "This isn't getting us anywhere." Being quicker to *jinx*, her point carried. "Tandy?" somebody piped up from another table, "if it weren't for him, *I'd* be out of a job. I daresay most of my friends would be as well." He was using a bearded Russian doll with domino teeth to crack walnuts. He'd sift the contents in his left palm, tipping the crude shell splinters into a Hobstar bowl from Corning. "Nobody I know has been to one of his upstate retreats in ages." "Retreat? Upstate? Sounds very 1940s." "Well, not everything about him is a throwback ..." Knocked out early, Mary drifted from match to match, conversation to conversation, without aim or interest—attracted by the nearest shiny object. "What's this?" she asked, picking up a newly purchased card still in the plastic sleeve—it looked like one of those from the downstairs tobacco and magazine shop. Mary had finally accepted the fact that the eighteen floors of their building seemed to be organized by age, with rare (incomprehensible, naturally) exceptions. Three floors beneath with tenants who seemed wet behind the ears, while the rest advanced above to the senility of the penthouse suites. The more she thought about it, the more disturbing this arrangement seemed. "You think they'll ask us to move up when we hit—?" "Are you nuts? Most of them have been here for years—you think they're all playing Tollhouse *tic-tac-toe*?" "But how can that be?" Mary said. "It doesn't make sense." "We've got to try to stop being so literal-minded," Doug said, "I know, I do it too, but it's got to stop. Agreed?" To stop thinking about the *literal* impossibility of the building's arrangement? She decided to agree. But that morning, while grabbing some breath mints on her way out, it hit her that over half the tobacconist's merchandise belonged in a hospital gift shop—children's and maternity. Tubs with roses, carnations, and tulips. The selection of overpriced cigars. Bunches of balloons, toys that took the pull of a string to talk, plush animals, etc. She'd also noticed a disproportionate selection of condolence cards. It reminded her, unpleasantly, of the arrangement of floors in the Tollhouse, a pattern of local development that could have worked only this once, *without repetition*, exactly when the Monadoons moved in. Doug made room for her on the edge of his footstool, and slanted his cards her way, ordered by suit. Among other things, he held high hearts and the Queen of spades. The reason behind his smirk. Couldn't anybody else see? She loved him then with an intensity that brought her up short. Furman led with a seven of diamonds, obviously fishing, and the pile picked up several hearts before Doug nabbed it with the King. "There sure are a lot of Toms on this floor," Mary said, and Belle, Tom Acres, Furman, and Emma all looked at her like she'd dropped a plate. "No more than statistical average," said Acres. "It's a very common name." "That it is," said Emma. "Do you sometimes feel you've been gypped?" "Not at all!" exclaimed Acres. "Never mind Tom," Belle interrupted—"Doug's trying to shoot the moon." Doug protested the young lady's sportsmanship, as he always did when caught out, and there was an intersection of voices, four at once, and laughter. People were holding their drinks well—picking them up and putting them down without creating new condensation rings. "You were on a roll tonight," Doug said as they made ready for bed. "Were you trying to get us forcibly removed? But it was wonderful, darling, really." "What?" Mary said, in all innocence. "Doug, what are you *talking* about?" He had started on her neck already, the place he felt most at ease devoting his attentions, and his fishlike nibbling was arousing in a special kind of way, perhaps because there was never the release . . . later, she stroked his member while it spied on her like a weary emperor. They spooned into sleep, his left arm safely about her waist. So when she woke the next day to discover him, and "I can't go" written in his blood on the bathroom mirror—in jets, smeared in—Mary's first thought was—*where*? Somebody was buzzing their doorbell. A brightly suited delivery guy. She signed for the package, then fainted. He'd made a hole in his throat with an exacto blade—obviously located the optimal point of entry. After writing his note on the central mirror, Doug had slipped and fallen facedown into the tub. She knew she would always see his blood on the faucets whenever she adjusted the *hot* or *cold* water. *Where* couldn't he go? The detectives asked her the same question. They asked other questions as well, all of which eventually led back to that one. She held herself in abeyance. She was in shock. She didn't know. She couldn't explain what she did know, because they wouldn't understand. *Love keeps perpetuating surprises or it dies*, Doug seemed to be telling her, not helpfully. They had been more than man and wife. They had been sweethearts. Everybody could see they were going to make it. When she returned to the apartment Doug had violated, the first thing she noticed was the package left unopened on the coffee table's glass countertop. Somebody had wrapped and tied it very nicely with yellow ribbon, although the card seemed lost. At least, Mary *thought* she could remember an envelope taped to it, which she had nonsensically assumed contained a condolence card . . .

Being inside Central Park was very different from what she expected, in that it felt no different from being outside. Disappointment was inevitable. When her nine-month-old daughter had been removed from her care for the sole crime of lacking a name, Mary looked deep within herself to find the strength at her core—she would let her inner unreason guide her, she decided. The condolence cards had poured in. Everybody in the building wrote her one, people she didn't know, names she'd never heard, but nobody pressed themselves on her or overstepped. Besides red velvet cake, she ate raw carrots, radishes, bergamots and snap peas. She organized the cards on mantels and countertops, wherever she could, each one an angel balancing on open wings. Occasionally, she would read what was inside. She cried so much she didn't need them, really, and then she retreated into winter hibernation—the docile double-womb for Mary and the daughter coming of age inside her—during which she read every one of the *Collected Short Stories* of John Cheever. She read them once in order, and then she started jumping around. She never learned who had given her the gift on that fateful day, but at the core of her unreason she believed it to be Doug. He'd ordered an advance copy before impulsively introducing himself to his maker and hoping for the best. The Park had been a fairy tale weaved in concert with some character out of a Cheever story. Deep down they'd both known it. Disappointment was inevitable. She read on park benches, tearing out the pages as she went and feeding them to the pigeons. *Let them choke on them.* A man sitting on the opposite end of the bench turned to speak, but the woman he addressed wasn't Mary. It sounded like Daisy or maybe Hazel. Hazel was the sort of name Mary wouldn't have minded for herself, and if—but now that she got a good look, he was obviously a transient. She stood up and walked south, quickly, down a rise, up a dell, to the spongelike oaks spaced around the Little

League diamonds. A team of sophomores seemed to be playing itself, boys rotating in from the field to bat. She watched for a while, noting that when three of the batters were deemed *out*, the players switched their fielding positions so as to create innings of a sort, and competition, until a foul ball landed several feet from her. Shuddering, she aimed herself across the Great Lawn, to a dwarf maple whose leaves had begun to catch. She kept glimpsing activity in her peripheral vision—which disappeared whenever she turned her head in its direction. The opposite of what one might expect, it was worse on the open lawn. Either that or the feeling was building the more time she spent inside the Park. Midtown's towers shot up from the skyline of trees south. After the fairy-tale castle feeding on the mildew of the lake, huffing and puffing around a blind corner of the Ramble, she ran into Doug in the guise of a middle-aged man. Later, he would explain that outside the park he aged one year to nine-and-a-half of her days. "And inside ... ?" Inside, he said, the situation was more or less the reverse. She had lots of questions. When he was beside her, when he touched her, what had been air was now filled with folks. Newly formed couples intent on communicating, mismatched lovers embracing and falling into one another's arms, into thin air, taking the final leap. She watched the children come and go beneath Conservatory Pond, right before the plaza narrowed into a single-lane defile down to the underground zoo. The women talking there almost insolently careless with their charges. Toddlers were exploring the ends of benches, spilling out of the circular openings of fungible cubes, rolling headfirst down plastic slides. "*We* are the children!" Mary said, suddenly benighted. "We were," said Doug ruefully, "not anymore." "Is that you?" Mary sniffed unkindly in his direction. "No," said Doug, "but the smell is maybe *related* to me." Always the sophist, even after the afterlife. "Why isn't our daughter here?" Mary asked. The Doug-who-was-old-enough-to-be-Mary's-father looked shocked. "What do you mean?" he said . . . "she's not dead, is she?" "No thanks to you!" "I believed it was for the best," he said, "you going forward with your life, me watching over you, to make sure everything's okay." "But it hasn't worked out like that at all!" "No . . ." he admitted. She told him about their daughter's birth and the agonies that had convinced her to go epidural. This pain preceded everything: word, world, woods. The prison walls of different heights that kept everything in the Park *inside.* They'd been living in one. It started in her back, but very quickly where it started didn't matter. She'd cried out to Doug, but he wasn't around, she told him bitterly. The inconceivable force of their daughter had erased his furtive exigencies once and for all, or so she'd thought, the pain of precedence making reason seem the most irrational labor of all. She could not endure above it or wrench free. In recovery, they'd told Mary it was a son. Just to confuse the issue. That whole summer they eroded her arguments with catheters and pills. Arguments? It was *why* or pleading. Then, when his turn came, Doug told her in awful detail about the compound eye he'd become part of. Only Mary could release him from the consequences of his mistake, he said, and then only temporarily, by entering this park they'd never visited together—not once —during his lifetime. "Or alone," she said. "Or alone," he agreed.

TAKEN/NOT TAKEN

When her grandfather passed on, he left Hannah in the care of an old woman who spent most of her time in bed, or occasionally turned sideways on the living-room sofa. Hannah knew her as Mrs. Riley, out of politeness, and over the many years she lived with the old lady and her grandson, never shifted to closer terms, not of affection, ridicule, or even habit. Genevieve, her given name, seemed out of step with the doughy, white-haired "guardian" introduced to Hannah at the Chase Family Funeral Parlor. And while there were old photos around the house, Mrs. Riley in her youth looked no more a Genevieve than the present Mrs. Riley. By no means a delicate flower—tomboyish, with sunburned skin, cropped curly hair, and a humorous, that's-enough-non-sense look, in stark contrast to the disconcerting way she stared out at people now. Narrow seating in a viewing room of dark wood, oak or imitation oak, pledged to a fresh lemon shine. The reception annex had more space, large soda bottles on the end tables, sweet and salty snacks in fancy glass bowls and goblets. There was a tall usher who didn't seem out of high school yet, with weak blue eyes and wet lashes, who kept glancing over at her. An old woman in black approached him, and he pointed Hannah out. That would have been her grandson, Aleister, unless he was some kind of "miracle baby"—a remote possibility that at times tickled Hannah's fancy. It explained a lot—the pair's secretive bonds for one thing, a closeness Hannah never penetrated in her years living under the same roof—never came close or wanted to, really. And "miracles" were happening every day, they said. The old woman sat next to Hannah, without asking permission or offering condolence—without speaking at all, in fact. A pouched redoubtable face, disclosing more pucker lines than wrinkles, with a whiskery complexion, very fine, silvery white hair, and noble eyebrows, black to grey—but her blue eyes seemed to belong to a different person—the eyes of an ecstatic. She remained behind when Hannah ascended the dais to pay her respects, then followed into the back room upholstered in human skin—no, it was perfectly ordinary, a green-and-yellow floral design on the wallpaper. A lawyer—and others who looked like they might be important—explained the situation to Hannah, "the transfer," with embarrassed pauses, as if waiting for Mrs. Riley to jump in. But beyond an initial introduction, she was all but mute. "Nan is extremely shy," Aleister had told her at her new home, once he'd escorted the old woman up to her bedroom, "and she tires easily. Maybe it would be easier if you communicated through me." She was nine years old at the time. Halfway through the fourth grade. At first she mistook Aleister's kindnesses, his punctilious solicitude, for some kind of clever manipulation. A common mistake, and one Aleister—a saint of small considerations—regarded with abstemiousness and forbearance. He was bullied relentlessly at school for being queer. They weren't wrong. There was something queer about him—superficially and down deep. He acted with Christian charitableness toward his persecutors, an almost gloating bending of the neck which, even before she "came of age," Hannah knew there was something disgraceful about. It wasn't that he encouraged the attacks, really, his appearance had to take most of the blame, Hannah thought: saddle-boned, rail-thin, with the face of a Raggedy Andy doll—thin red lips, chalky complexion, a button nose, eyes of diluted blue and eyelashes so wet they made the other parts, like the lips, seem wet or greasy themselves—elongated, or stretched thin, along the vertical axis, like a balloon that has started to deflate. He was striking-looking—but in a fairly repulsive way. His looks—the doll's face, in particular—gave him a different perspective from other people, attuned to small kindnesses, to politeness as a holy shield, if not a weapon at times. Of course, he had morbid attachments as well. That first meeting, he'd just begun at the funeral parlor, it couldn't have been more than a few days as an intern on an irregular stipend—but even then he knew. This was his vocation, what he was meant to do. The smells made his eyes water—but he acknowledged them, along with the odd noises, as the final pronouncements of the otherwise evacuated flesh. Not bothered by the bodies buried inside other bodies—nor their uncouth substrates. "What did your grandma think?" Hannah asked him. "Nan? Oh, I don't bother her with stuff like that!" he said. It was a perfect fit for Aleister and the Chase family, particularly for the Chases, who contemptibly exploited Aleister's drive and talents, one special one above all, without giving him the position or salary he was due. People entering a funeral parlor are naturally prone to anger or hate, whatever target is close. The Chases must have seen it at once, Aleister's peculiar capacity for deflecting anger onto himself—gossamer yet a startlingly *effective* gravitational field—making their own dealings with the bereaved that much more pleasant. On every performance review, however, they made sure to inform him of his dismal customer ratings—how could he hope to get ahead with such numbers? So looks it was. The old shell game—how many rebuffs and retreats could he manage and still remain par? It was his whole life. She remembered how he'd ump for the games of Kick the Can she would play with other neighborhood kids her age, until a couple of the parents complained. She remembered him making a joke of it— "well, we knew *that* wouldn't last"—which only made her mistrust him more. Call it the snowball effect—he took it and took it and never made a fuss, right up to the day of his death, a hit and run they said, two years after Mrs. Riley's own passing from a chill turned irreparable, when Hannah was twenty-six—and still to her dismay in B—and she was alone again.

She still fondly remembered the games played during those long summer twilights. They favored a parcel of birch and oak projecting out of the imperial woodlands behind the backyard tracts, between the Hunt and Snyder yards. After bending right, Magnolia Drive quickly dead-ended, pavement to gravel to the chest-high grass and cattails of a park-sized meadow. The can—ideally with its label torn off—was planted upside-down on the curb next to the Hunt lawn. There'd been lots of arguments about where the can should fairly sit—on the curb, in the gutter, where the pavement crumbled, different driveways—and Aleister had listened to all sides and found a compromise surprisingly suited to and even exceeding everybody's wishes. He winked at her when he set it down—which she didn't like. "Kick the Can," she said, later—he was fixing her a raisin, fluff, and jelly sandwich, "you used to play yourself." "No, Hannah, not exactly," he replied, "I was permitted to watch—I took notice." But the location he extrapolated out of their complaints (or stolen from past games) was all right. It was more than all right. The wedge or copse created an ideal—if easily spotted—vantage from which to view the base camp. Trying to hide out there—

crawl or dash for cover, standing stiff as a board behind some puny birch—was a great temptation—dangerous under normal circumstances, and all but impossible once the seeker had caught and "turned" others to his or her side. She loved the black-&-white boundaries of worlds that began in games, no hesitations, no loyalty questions, none of nature's compromises—undifferentiated man-made constructions. You get tagged, you change sides. It's that simple. The birch trees weren't great cover, but their black-&-white bark like parchment fascinated Hannah. Even the youngest had the skin of some useless relic. The broad lap of lawn—a triangular no-man's-land between the two neighbors, with the woods wedged into its apex—threadbare willow oak, a shaving-brush spinney of birch, shrubbery with moats of dark turf chemicals—down which they'd charge in formation or ragtag, legs free and hearts pounding, or the other way, alone or in company, dodging their captors, racing for the can—all in. The cicadas would unleash their sonic static not at a regular time, but during a particular change in the density of the evening light. Aleister had taught her that, and she'd taught herself to recognize that particular transition—aquamarine to a lighter meringue shade. No, he didn't *teach* so much as inform her—politely shared some information in his possession. At what point fireflies start up is more erratic, he admitted—when she asked, and at age ten, she believed this was his way of saying he didn't know. More commonly, his politeness—the dictates of his overfed conscience—led him to withhold confidences and counsel, which made it harder in turn for Hannah to surrender her early suspicions. But she was young and the house she found herself in strange, in habit and air. The three-bedroom with attached garage seemed haunted. Otis was the most likely culprit, a young man with a long face, dolorous, puppy-dog eyes and cancer-infected lips, drawn in chalk on the basement wall near the washer and dryer. In truth, the lips could have been a defect in the drawing, or smudging. Mrs. Riley—whose presence was also a kind of haunting—communicated rarely, or the rareness was Aleister's doing, conveying only the matters he thought wouldn't trouble Hannah, she being so recently bereaved and so young. Too fragile. His consideration had unintended consequences, however. When he did issue "requests" (extremely gently) on his grandmother's behalf—generally pertaining to noise, Mrs. Riley's hearing having become *more* intent with age it seemed—they would come to Hannah freighted with potentially life-altering consequences and thus throw her into a panic. And then—almost in the same instant—*resentment*! Things creaked—clocks chimed—all through the house! How could her walking up the stairs be any different? The banister stopped at the ceiling, while the stairs continued through a narrower cutaway to the second floor—sometimes she'd pretend it was sea-level and play mermaid, "swimming" up the stairs to surface in the faded orange lagoon of a bedroom-bracketed hallway, and the "medicine closet" smelling weirdly like Aleister. Games at home were for one—she had a hard time persuading others to visit—even Rebecca Reynolds, her best friend at the new elementary, who wasn't ashamed to share the toilet with Hannah whichever number her business. Vandalism was a problem throughout the year, but especially when the leaves changed, up to Halloween—and, certainly, nobody with any sense or social standing would enter their dismal abode. Speaking of Aleister, Becky told Hannah that just tempting people was evil, which is what Aleister did on a regular basis—provoke evil behavior—just like Damien the Antichrist, so his *conscious* motives—whatever they were—were more or less irrelevant. Becky with the overbite—in high school, she blossomed into kiss-and-tell royalty, dropping out and marrying young to a mean, compulsively possessive tight end for the Golden Bears. In grade five, however, she'd loved to read and collect Little Lulu comic books—they obsessed her instead of dolls. And Hannah didn't mind so much. She didn't really mind Becky's bossiness either. She'd gulp down the fresh-made lemonade (powder from a can) proffered by Rebecca's uncle, "Wren"—slovenly pours from a clinking plastic pitcher while she sat on one of two matching living-room sofas—Ethan Allen style— and admired the paint-by-numbers landscapes decorating the walls, or pretending to. She didn't have an opinion one way or the other. It did seem a nice *normal* hobby, however. And she'd return from play, indoors or out, to 646 Magnolia Drive—the tomblike air, the dead or absent adults, the devoted grandson, the creaks, chimes and hollow wind sounds—with a heaviness of despair she could never wriggle out from under. Although Mrs. Riley seemed older than her years, whatever they were, she wasn't a frail woman exactly. Her vicinity carried an acrid pee-and-sweat tang which kept Hannah at a distance even when Mrs. Riley did venture downstairs. But it was more than that. The old lady didn't move the way other people did—on a spectrum of continuities. She seemed to gain brief access to circulation, forcing her to act fast and with a minimum of fuss, every gesture and movement rehearsed or at least planned in advance, and therefore somewhat robotic. Like a child hopping onto a merry-go-round. Once this analogy came, Hannah wouldn't let go—the old lady's stillnesses seemed like watching for the right pole or animal part to grab onto. Hannah was always somewhat uneasy around her guardian, but the period of active mistrust (and this applied to Aleister as well) ended the day Mrs. Riley told Hannah about her experiences above. It was like a revelation . . . before and after as neatly compartmentalized as black and white. It put lots of things into perspective. After his wife had been taken, Hannah's granddad succumbed to the slow inertia of the outwitted survivor, grinding to a halt, losing his few remaining students, running up debt, increasingly confused, passive and self-destructive until one day he stuck his head in the oven and released the gas, not caring who found him.

Having finished 90 percent of the dialog in a Ritalin-inflected blur, she writes out a set of stage directions for her one-act, *I Scream for Ice Cream.* The year is 1974. The scenery puts one in mind of upstate New York. Trees may include magnolia, oak, maple, and birch, plenty of the last, all bare. In winter the stands of birch don't seem as stranded as the rest somehow. Billy and his former landlady are grappling with life-and-death matters on a minimalist stage. There is a chorus behind them and in the wings, wordless, holding hands to mouths, clutching chests or solid things within easy reach. Lynn O'Reilly knows that if she flinches for half a second, Billy's going to do it. She knows that if she just twitches in the direction of the people behind her, the boy's going to do it. She calls on God and Jesus both to keep her strong so she can save Billy, who is kneeling in the marked fore-quadrangle of the stage, while she stands in her chalked paces, hands crossed and pressing against the lapels of her dressing gown. "Turn around!" he pleads, when the play opens in *medias res,* "shut your ears!" Is there also a *meta* appeal to the people who've come to watch? Billy Doherty will be pleading with his former landlady (he hasn't lived with Patti for some time). His motivations are alluded to during the action of the play, which happens fast once it starts, but never "spelled out." Hannah decides to include them in her stage directions for the actors to incorporate into their performances, or acknowledge at their discretion. For example, in the parts where she allows them to "talk at will." Ken Rosslyn, the Artistic Director of the Cider Mill Playhouse, makes his unhappiness about these improvised moments known, calling it lazy, and the play—by implication—unfinished. *Talk at will.* God forbid. When the lights go up, Billy has just blown off a chunk of another guy's head. One determines this indirectly because Billy's the only one up on stage with a gun. He is squatting with the handle of a twelve-gauge on the ground, the barrel wedged beneath his talking chin, and at different times, his weeping forehead. The action is Mrs. O'Reilly trying to talk him out of suicide until, about twenty minutes to half an hour in (depending on the improvisations), she starts to ask herself *why* she's trying to save this terrifying man, and Billy, who is a bad person but good at reading other people's faces, pulls the trigger, and the stage goes black around the sound of the gunshot. Hannah wants no curtain call, but Rosslyn exercises his veto.

This is what Hannah knows to have happened, but which can't be expressed within the written part of the exchange—only prepared for. As a rule, she likes to compress her writing of dialog into the time it would take to speak the words—*real time* more or less, to give it the freshness and continuity of improvisation. In a sense, her plays are all variations on *if only I had* . . . she's pared down the X from schemes and addictions, to the things people said, or wish they had, even an absence of doing or, as in this case, a way of looking, regarding herself as note-taker, merely, for the voices dredged up—the people Bearden County releases from her unconscious. He'd meant to shoot Patti, for her lies and infidelities both known and mysterious to him, but Amadou Ba had sprung for the stock, or the barrel, and Billy had taken his life instead. It looks as red as the syrup smeared on in films. There's a crater on the skull, which is difficult for Billy to look near, to see what he's done, impossible to know by accident or with intent. Either way, it was very spur of the moment. It didn't matter. He knew he was responsible. He knew he was going to hell. Hannah had taken the basics from news accounts of the incident, altering names and motivations slightly. She wanted stories with some bite to them—stories with teeth. Rosslyn, however, proves a real pain in the ass—a total process guy—opinionated, incorruptible, easily led up or down the garden path. What about Mr. Ba? He was from Mali. He worked at World of Sound, as an appliance salesman—rented downstairs from Billy's estranged wife, Patti, with whom he'd been on familiar terms, Billy suspected, as he dwelled on the matter—more and more, the more time they spent apart. Her infidelity with a man of Mali, a Muslim. This guy had the childish formality and polite bearing of a foreigner learning the language, but that didn't make him white. Billy always was crazy jealous. Patti had said it to him time and again. "So why'd you go out with me?" he'd answer, "knowing what you are." "Says you," she'd say, sometimes bitter, sometimes in anger, sometimes sad, but never accepting the fault as her own. Like it was his doing mostly. "I guess it was my bad luck then," he said. He'd imagined it different, of course. His anger fed a permissive point of view—he'd shoot the grin off her cheating face. He'd thought about it often, but stopped confiding these thoughts to others—given the looks he was beginning to get—except sometimes a stray word or comment would slip out, whenever he got loaded. He'd blast those lips that lied and sucked every white and nigger cock in sight. It was already the case when he met her—but she got away from him, with the two kids, their eyes bulging like they were battery-operated. He had been preparing to kill them too. What the fuck. He'd kill them all, then kill himself, he'd decided. Violence casts an unreal spell on the mind conceiving it, it becomes something that needs to be renewed, over and over again, just to feel normal.

Things hadn't changed much by the time Hannah entered community college—Aleister had a title at Chase's, but of the lowest grade, and he still lived at home with her and Nan. Hannah was encouraged to stay on herself, until she could afford her own place...if that was what she wanted. She had to know she could stay as long as she wanted, the house being as much hers as theirs. "And—well, you know how good we are at keeping out of your way," Aleister added. But he understood how much she wanted to flee the doldrums of Bearden. They'd talked about it often enough—while watching clouds cross the county. Aleister would treat her to picnics once a fortnight in the spring, summer and early fall (winters they'd "hibernate," as he put it). In time, she'd come to see they were as much for his sake as hers, more—interrupting the slow pounce of loneliness on boredom, however briefly—and this made her feel sad and strangely guilty. The east slope of Bunn Hill was a favorite spot—for some reason, ants avoided it. He would bring home-cut slices of baloney with iceberg and mayo on wonderfully soft bread, stacked potato chips, cracker-and-cheese packets, soda, and Pop Rocks for dessert. It was a rare instance of thoughtlessness on Aleister's part (Hannah had grown out of this kid's fare a long time ago), or a nostalgia she was happy to submit to. They lounged in a canal of cut grass between pylons. The pylons were still linked in those days, they hadn't retreated from Willow Point—the button-side of one green against another hill's loosened collar. She told Aleister all about her plans for escape because she knew it was harmless—as if their county didn't lap at the heels of the metropolis east. Two shakes for a commute. Sometimes he would let her go on, sometimes remonstrate or argue—always gently, of course. "How could I leave," he asked rhetorically, "when everything and everybody I know is here—Nan, you, the Chases, the kids I grew up with, who are all married now—it's so *interesting* to see how they've paired up!—their uncles and kin, my colleagues, your friends." He talked about the special porousness between past and present in a place like B—, in a county like Bearden, blessed by its many famous pockets where ghosts could sneak through in unusually high numbers, their ancestors and the other anchors that kept him here—willingly, Aleister said, happily. "We can't abandon them, can we? I mean for our own sakes, if not for theirs." A remote buzzing in the air. Insects? Or messages from the pylons framed overhead? "What's that one look like?" he asked, keeping his finger pointed while she attempted to follow its trajectory, up—into the acquiescent blue. "I'm not sure," she said, looking at the wrong cloud, obviously. "Recognizing yourself in the mirror of your kids, that must be sobering," Aleister said. "And if things go wrong, a nightmare. I can imagine—*almost*. It changes you, they say—that sort of recognition. Now imagine—just try—how it is for *them*." One out of a thousand taken, and of those maybe one in seven returned. Clouds posted like uncanny harbingers, refusing to make room for their ominous-looking cousins wanting in from outside . . .

Only later does the chorus come to light.... The *Evening Press* gives *I Scream for Ice Cream* a negative review—very rare in the fragile theater ecology of the Triple Cities area and an unbelievable first for a Cider House Production—and while Rosslyn seethes, his company "besmirched" by the low quality of the play, Hannah views it as a badge of honor. These days everything is horror movies, the reviewer complains, citing *The Omen, Beyond the Door, The Sentinel,* and *The Power of One,* and it's a shame this no-longer-young-exactly local talent (he cites *Lindsay at Large*) should have hopped on the bandwagon. "My ears are still ringing from the predictable conclusion," he writes—and why not? Mediocrity is the way they wall up the county. Country productions of Gilbert & Sullivan, regionalized Strindberg for the daring. Dawn arrives on rosy fingers. House lights behind the assembled flats, or the other way around. Now there's more light rising from either side of the stage, which has gotten very crowded. The preparatory-to-dawn presence of a three-story townhouse, as indicated by backdrop or projection—and the presence of snow. The thing itself isn't a memory, although it appears to be stored in the same part of her brain, lodged behind or underneath, and yet much smaller than even the hinted memory of childhood—microscopic by comparison, making it harder to isolate and get rid of, a sense of premonition Hannah loans to Mrs. O'Reilly, named "premonition" only because it's so black-&-white obvious. Every time Billy "dropped by" to speak with her—... he was an appalling person, and she had to listen, appalled, to the opinions he entrusted her with—just as he accepted her rebukes and exclamations of horror and requests that he not say such things in front of her, meekly bowing his head as he would before his own mother, but without amending his behavior even slightly. He'd apologize and go right on being crazy. *Let me speak!* They're right on top of her. So is Billy, in a sense. She was—they were—watching the country they'd grown up in vanish before their eyes, with nothing to replace it except these pockets of dead air. Fame or death, death or fame. It *can't* be dangerous to talk of such things. And what if it is—? Freedom *should* be a little bit dangerous. "Okay okay okay . . . let me just *think* for a second . . ."

The ground is soaked from the ice and sleet, the river is still rising. It rises behind the backyards, and below, lumpy but moving fast, the color of dirt in the half-morning light. Talk about will. Somehow Amadou Ba's death—a stupid mistake—keeps him here, for the present, in the worst county of the most terrifying country imaginable. The different states of America. He tries to explain why he's late for his shift, but the manager won't hear him out—no, they're going to have to "let him go." Her uncle's farm was on the same river, the Susquehanna, and as a child Mrs. O'Reilly used to worry about the water coming up and carrying them all off. A white screen towers over the roof-shaped flats. The center stage darkens while porches and garages appear indistinctly on the screen, in the pre-dawn. The chorus becomes more focused on the sky as it begins to lighten, imperceptibly adjusting to the rheostat—radio alarms go off, ads on Mix 103.3—how do the sponsors manage to time it right every morning? "Powerful growth formula—now with more free olyoxin than ever!" Lights pop on, up and down the stage. Patti screams, is screaming inside to herself, then lets it out—she yells, but someone silences her. One homeowner—who's just finished a cup of coffee and two pieces of whole-wheat toast with low-calorie marmalade—is about to pick up a scuffed briefcase and go out when he returns to his living room and sits before an upright piano with kids' practice books sprawled on the rack. He flexes his fingers and starts playing Liszt's *Liebesträume*—adds a few notes to the cadenza, allowing a piano roll. The stage fills with music, then fades away while the man looks down at his watch—a heavy, defeated character of six decades and change, wearing a plaid jacket with Bic ballpoints in the upper right pocket. He gets up, turns off the light that's hardly needed anymore. He goes out the door—down the porch steps. In Hannah's world, this is Marty Metzger. The precip's having trouble making up its mind, rain vacillating with sleet with ice flecks and even flakes of snow. The bushes begin to shake, but it's only the morning freight. Two come daily, blocking the main thoroughfare in his burb for ten minutes at least, three engines pulling the history of their bigger republic in trains—Union Pacific shackled to a Conrail car, Conrail to Sante Fe, Sante Fe to Soo Line, Soo Line to the Lackawanna, Lackawanna to Burlington North, Burlington North to Southern Pacific—it's a mystery how they all come to be conjoined, twenty-three cars snaking along slowly, paralleling the river, then crossing it on its own trestle bridge, which the more daring kids will use as a diving platform in the summer—then slowly moving on, through farm and hinterlands, the engines making strickened bird noises, which sometimes echo back, as if they're answering one another. A year eternal in heaven's spotlight. What of that? The reporter is describing his nights on the road with B—'s most famous "fame hunter." His rough-and-ready crew drive the nights through—the darker the better, clouds and storms are also helpful—in an off-road pickup with an enormous spotlight in back, which they direct at a 65-degree angle upwards, with somebody swiveling it in a 360-degree circle, trying to spy clues to changes in the density of the air. "It's like something jumping into your peripheral vision," says one of the hunter's assistants. "Or out," says another. "Yeah, either way." A tingle in the spine—a sixth sense—anything uncanny may apply, whereas there is no simple (*proven*, rather) scientific explanation. The pockets move around, apparently, and because they are "imperceptible" to the naked human eye (a fact the hunters dispute), documentary evidence is hard to come by. Many on the news believe it to be a hoax, or claim as much—a "traveling" version of the Bermuda Triangle mystery. Some astrophysicists believe it has to do with a "wobble" (in layman's terms) in the earth's axis-rotation, or so Dr. Sagan explains to the listening public, producing "tender spots"—atmospheric pockets where the gravitational force is reduced —and, in rare instances, "levitation effects." Reports of people shooting straight to the stars, however, are greatly exaggerated, says Dr. Sagan, chuckling at some people's credulity. But many ordinary residents—especially those in Bearden, who've been visited by more than their fair share—know better. It's a form of communication. Two-way. This is where the term "fame" comes in. It's a broadcast channel which people get accidentally caught up into—teleporting where? Problem is all the survivors, if that's even the word, have different accounts. "The ratio of those taken in Bearden is 1 to 177. For the country as a whole, it's more like one in a million." "That's a big difference." "Yes it is." "Does your *fame hunter* have any explanation why?" "No—in fact, he says it's none of his business. And none of ours." "He does? Well, he's certainly a character." "Yes, he is." "Thanks, Jim. That was a very informative story." "Yes, it was literally eye-opening."

Mr. Metzger wants music not metaphysics, but when he switches to the listener-supported station, he's defeated once again—"We interrupt our program for an important news bulletin." The same grief every time. Each loss lends motive, sends ripples through B—'s closely woven community, Hannah observes, in the only way her childhood could have taught her, once the Rileys had taken her in. Where does the stage world end and the real begin? Are we the poor players history's greatest playwright supposed us to be? She never did escape. The oncoming blur her grandfather's wipers clear every few seconds. He shifts into neutral, coasts down the exit ramp, hooking a right onto Hallam while ignoring a pair of yellows flashing "caution"—passes a corridor of caved-in structures bookended by two derelict factories, the smaller one with an intact ziggurat of fire stairs dangling off the back. Here the road narrows into the two lanes of the Parkway Bypass. For approximately a half-mile west—the small wilderness separating the county seat in B— from the concatenated drag of Telemachus—it follows the river, bound to its slow turns ... He'd woken at dawn, yet here he was. Late again for his 10:30—by more than 15 minutes. Janet Loomis spared him the glance at her watch—and pointed to the alcove where he could peel off his galoshes. Grit and gravel on the linoleum—and that flash-powder salt would produce within a three-feet radius. He went down to his lesson. A Yamaha piano kept out of tune by the dampness of the basement. Mrs. Loomis's charge—the relation so distant it was confusing to explain, she said—was guiltily making up for the practice he'd neglected every day of the past week by reproducing "By the Rushing River" with a ratio of right-to-discordant notes that summoned and sullenly intertwined the complex miseries of both teacher and student. Mr. Martin started him on scales. They'd set the Yamaha flush to the wall opposite the stairs, behind a couch and television set-up, kitty-corner from a disused bar counter now piled with old magazines. He shared the bench with young Walter too intent on his hands—standing every so often to iron out any cramping. "Where does that door go?" he asked the boy, interrupting the scales trotted out arrhythmically. "It doesn't go anywhere." "What do you mean?" "Check it out if you don't believe me." "Of course I believe you, Walter. What do you think you'd like to learn next? 'Walk With Me' or 'Greensleeves'?" "Hmm—I don't know either one." "Haven't heard 'Greensleeves'! Well then, that's where we'll start." This whole time Mr. Martin had been inching toward the door. He had to rotate the teeny pommel counterclockwise—vertical to horizontal—to get it open and confirm for himself the boy was right. A crawlspace or sort of spandrel the height of a child bisected a dozen or so steps knocking up against the garage floor. "That's odd," said the piano teacher— "why didn't they push through to make an exit?"

"I had the worst thought—I wanted to talk to you, explain, before—I don't remember getting took—the whole *year* before's lost, my teens foggy as well, but that's normal, the normal, I—you'll . . . get to my age and you'll see, it isn't all cream and roses—Alice, carmel please—sorry for the trouble . . . I remember being a little girl better than anything— . . . wish I knew why, it would help to understand, I think. There's so much I can't account for—I—that's age I, oh—shit almighty— but it's something else, something I don't want to understand—the length of travel, leaping star to—that's my recurring nightmare every time you close your eyes— you don't mind if I close mine for a while, do you, child? To fight it, to move, Alice—would you . . . ? But that's not the same thing as—oh no—and when I arrived (a lifetime in itself), I—the one who'd been taken—they were frightened of *me!* All of them, rather, all the ones who could actually *see* me were—but of *me!* Of me! But I was the one lost. Why had they abducted me? And were they even the ones responsible? It doesn't seem like it, now ... later—now and later I didn't think so ... so you see it looked like a spaceship—hulls, corridors, compartments clean as a whistle... lots of white space—now I— look there, Alice, yes, thank you, thank you, you're so good to me ... but my expectations made it so, now I— living in hiding from—and you know what? These alien beings—they were *all human!* It was like a dream, exactly like a dream, but I couldn't wake up and I couldn't make any of them perceive me, or when they did—the slow ones—understand ... but—and whenever I got close to one, I'd get this tingling... then a vertigo like I'd run out of air—I couldn't—it's—I—" The hurtling momentum of a bad fall that goes on and on. The longer it did, without her recovering her senses (which, in effect, meant returning *here*), the more this dream of falling became her reality, inviting her to share its false views and beliefs. Placed within quotes, the old woman's manner might seem flustered, but that wasn't how she spoke—

long pauses like she was choosing her words with care, but when she did, it was rapid and robotic, the same way she moved. Whoever plays Hannah's guardian should regard the periods, question marks and exclamations as two-second pauses, dashes four, and ellipses six, at least—but she should play the commas *as is*, retaining their thin filigree of delay, or erratic detachment. She would evince a sort of gnomic satisfaction when she got a phrase or longer out—more often she'd get stuck on a pronoun, first- or second-person. The actual voice gruff, the congestion getting worse as she unwound. Cosmonauts monitored the ship—again she believed this to be her projection—anachronistic slippage. They had on unisex outfits resembling Fruit of the Loom underwear, webbed very fine yet not at all transparent, covering their entire bodies and leaving only an oval for the face—a human face every time—to occupy. The ship itself was congested. When she first arrived, nobody could see her, but whenever they got close, the pull of their mental gravity, transient auras, present companies, pheromone-like processes, invisible force fields, antimatter shields (it could have been any of these things, Hannah's guardian said) made her very sick. It took her a long time to describe this illness. It was like static electricity but worse. It was worse than getting an electric shock. She couldn't make them see her, nor explain her—their—predicament, but if she was careful, she could listen in to their conversations, because not only were they human, they spoke American-accented English, and many could even have grown up in the northeast corridor. All things considered, this disturbed Genevieve more than actual aliens. They'd go on and on about the awful experiment performed on humankind—in secret, of course—using words like "contact shock" and "deceleration." The last was a favorite of the cosmonauts ... one in particular—a kind of medical officer. After a while, probably due to the unseemly repetition of the word, Genevieve noticed a few of the passengers strikingly different from the rest. The slow ones. At first they seemed like storeroom dummies, extremely well-modeled dummies—meaning they could just as easily have been androids turned off or in hibernation mode—who kept to their private quarters. Over time she realized they did move, but whether so slowly as to be imperceptible to the naked eye or whenever she wasn't around or looking, she never did discover. Once she got herself oriented and could manipulate the ship's controls—all responded to her touch, surprisingly—

Genevieve felt she could reduce the dangers of "contact shock" (she borrowed this term from the cosmonauts—what *else* could it mean?) by attempting to share living quarters with these slower passengers. But her attempts to make existence on board a bit more comfortable led to further horrors. For these slow ones were the only cosmonauts capable of noticing her presence—and for some reason it *terrified* them. She discovered how erratic, unreasoning and infectious fear can be when molded into the stillnesses they had obtained, at least within her viewing. The first time she'd woken with fingers planted mere inches from her neck—lifted to strangle—and the expression immobilized on that face! Sheer ecstatic terror—hers was just as great. As she told Hannah all this, in that stifling, robotic way of hers, suddenly Hannah realized the old lady was able to talk only when she herself wasn't moving. "*He* was doing it, the medical officer, how many lifetimes did it take me to find that out? Changing them, one by one, slowing them down, until he'd be the only normal one left. For what possible purpose? I never did find out, never rescued—it didn't matter, really, the 'ship'—the thing I was entombed in, like all of the other frightened cosmonauts, this repulsive medical officer included—buried in the unknown grave of far space—I couldn't even get a bead on whether we were still in the same galaxy—was some sort of organism, and it was alive—...no...even worse, it was *human!* It was this living, breathing, thinking, corrupting *human* thing, which was taking us farther and farther into space!" Here Hannah had to interrupt—"You mean you were being hosted inside its body?" "No," said the old lady in an agony of congestion, and then she said something extraordinary—"Oh, god!"—and she repeated this exclamation, almost mindlessly, or without paying it any mind, while slipping in somewhere, *as its thoughts*—"—ohgod!ohgod!ohgod—!!"

All his life he'd known she would be taken from him—married life, if there was a distinction. The feeling seemed to bend and blur beyond mere facts, coloring even his childhood. Certainly, she'd filled the hole inside him. Gerald Martin's need for love. Mary. Mary Waters was everything he'd wanted in a girl—a wholesome, heart-melting handful—and she knew it, knew it because he'd confessed it on their first date, in so many words. Presumptuously (and preemptively, she'd figured) and then thought, what the hey, for she never swore, she might as well make his life impossible seeing that, without her, it would all be one big lie anyway. His "bad feeling" significantly intensified with the strange news—they'd interrupted Schubert's *Fantasia for piano and violin* to inform him—a high-priority premonition. A former student. What made a person do such things? What was he trying to tell them? God only knew. That day the sleet switched to snow and never looked back— a parade of soft strangers persevering in their white drift down from above—a blizzard—stuck, and without the means to carry itself out of their chain of low valleys— for five days. And that was to date. Still more was being promised. The Susquehanna had breached its banks, so- liciting minor property damage—households he vis- ited, or had at some time, temporarily evicted. Was there a connection? Was it a sign? In any case, he could hardly explain to Mary *why* he'd been moody all week. She'd nagged him about the battery—warned him, in fact— and now he was paying the price. It had died on his way back from the Rudins' niece and nephew up Bunn Hill way, when he'd pulled into the Present Company at the bottom of the hill, to grab some eggnog for Mary. He ag- onized over a Hummel merry wanderer, but couldn't get past the price—$6.99 in a size he could buy at the mall for a dollar and a half less. Or the same amount but a size up. His first thought was that the car, linked to Mary telepathically, was punishing him for his cheapness. Too cold to fool around with cables, so he locked up and left it where it was, snug enough, to be buried in the parking lot. Through dunelike drifts—into the dusklike grey—a diagonal stamp toward the crown of Imperial Drive—powder reached the tops of Gerald Martin's galoshes, or just about. An adult and child were practicing the snowplow, the little one a wobbly star on short skis, the adult first, going down backwards, with arms bracingly outstretched. By jackets alone he couldn't tell who. There were so many different guardians in their tract. Trucks with orange rotating lights salted and cleared the Parkway, churning up a wake of brown snow. The snowflakes looked so lawful under the arc lights of the Present Company—an enormous eggshell-colored warehouse, one story—the way they fell in serious, strict, solemn order. But what a mess they caused! He clapped his gloves, writhed his shoulders, hunched, hugging himself. The air pulled at his lungs like a string, and he stumbled before reaching the base of the tract, where the less tutored homes were situated. Same siding—the vinyl just a bit shabbier. It was late for Christmas lights, but the Caputos still had theirs up, blinking out of order—red, yellow, blue, and green decorating the icing that restored eaves, hedges, garages to their purely ideal states. Children were out playing in nearly every yard, and in the streets, enjoying the snow day. A week of snow days—"a whole *week!*" his daughter's little girl cried amazed, listening to the radio every morning, the cry a way of pinching herself. The endless benison *was* a dream of sorts, and the sky had the sort of grey found in his earliest ones, in harmony with the TV's elusive static, pushed out—from quietly illuminated dens—just so far. Chestnut provided the best run for the Flexible Flyers with their sleek rails and ambidextrous steering, looping east to take the big hill's gradients in steps, with curves both tight and wide, long straightaways and steep drops, while Magnolia was one funneled plunge to the bottom. This was where the younger kids sledded, in their roll-up toboggans and silver saucers, the latter spinning into the big drifts that cushioned both sides of the road, making serious accidents all but impossible. On both roads, a layer of tire-lipped slush over densely packed snow. Humping through one exhaust-blackened groove, Gerald Martin noted it wasn't slush, in fact—more this damp, heavily sifted flour—and wondered whether the hundreds of Eskimo words for snow included differences in texture, and decided some must. In one encampment—near the entrance of an igloo with a tree for chimney—a little boy was working to attract attention to a lost glove, howling the forlorn as only children know how or why. "Hey grandpa!" another little one yelled. She was a girl. He turned around—and got the snowball right in his chest. His mood changed, instantly—he forgot about his premonition, the sense life was passing him by—and reached for a handful of perfect packing powder in response. The gang of cheerful hooligans "outgunned" him through sheer numbers, but he got a few good shots in, and they begged him to take them on as King of the Mountain, using the fortifications built by repeat visits of county plows. He worried about his energy, his vertigo, his arthritis, but after a while relented. Once precariously mounted, he worried he was too heavy—he'd sink or go crashing through the crust, maybe into the kids' fantasy of tunnels below. But the ramparts held him. The snow had stiffened up there, into a texture like fiberboard, and it made a satisfying crunch—like biting into the white center of an infinite gobstopper—against his boot heels. The year was 1974.

A VISIT TO THE SECOND FLOOR

Over time the shape of things gets harder and harder to disentangle from the shadow. Last night I was paid a visit by two friends from my childhood. I'd all but forgotten Alex and Eleanor, even though she'd been my first (and, in a sense, only) real love. First loves! High-school crushes get all the press, but try it when you're eight and illiterate ... functionally illiterate, that is. They'd lived several houses up from mine, in an identical plot. Brother and sister, did I mention that? She was roughly my age, though she acted more grown-up and "in charge" than me or her brother, when he was in fact the oldest by three years. But he deferred to her, and me he treated like an equal. For a year or more, we'd been inseparable. Him: a skinny-flabby boy with sharp features and red-rimmed green eyes. He had terrible allergies, I remember. Her: stringy brown hair, lanky-sinewy, and ugly-pretty, which is the only type of pretty that exists for me. Her brows hinted at an early gray and were cleft in such a way to make her look cross, which she often was—prone to fits of outrage and exasperation by the obstinacy of her brother, and me especially. I enjoyed setting her off. There was nothing I liked better, in fact. It was her air of entitlement that did it, I suppose, acting like the *chosen* leader while lacking any real facility in that area—being both strong-willed and extremely mercurial—and under her tutelage, or direction, so to speak, I learned the role of "instigator," not a natural inclination, though I grew into it. Bad habits never truly die. The scenarios of these games of our misspent childhood elude me now, there were so many—of Eleanor's invention mainly, but meant to cater to our ideas of fun, however clumsily. Hiding alone was a staple. Finding the most cramped spots to contract into, pretending not to breathe. I would play along, after token resistance, meanwhile plotting some minor or major treachery with Alex, who'd always balk at the last minute, when we were all set to wreck her plans. What would Eleanor do? Usually not talk to me for a time. How effective was her reproach? Pretty effective . . . you see, I had the crazy idea that the pair of us shared a secret rapport, communicating through the oblivious medium of Alex. Brown eyes. She had brown eyes. She had thin lips, meager almost, but with a pronounced philtrum she'd inevitably chew at, as if the angel who'd touched her there lingered for a while. Sure enough, although whip-smart, Eleanor was utterly lacking in higher wisdom, the "nectar of self-awareness" written about in the *Vedas*. She didn't blush easily, but when she did the pink went all the way up to her cheeks' highest points. It wasn't like I'd made careful study of her, oh no—I'd only learned how to worship at her feet. Recovering from my shock, I went to the kitchen cabinet and broke open a 14-year-old Clynelish I'd been saving for this very occasion, without realizing it—I poured neat and generous into some dusty shot glasses, and made the first toast, and we clinked, breathed in the mossy aroma, and drank. With the bottle at hand, we were caught up in no time. Alex, to my surprise, had turned out the ambitious one: a collection of business phrasings, two short novels praised for their playful surrealism, and a "Penguin Lives" of the twentieth-century English eccentric David Lindsay. "Want to know what the hardest part was?" he asked— "*the clothes!*" Throughout the biography, Alex found himself unable to write without picturing the clothes the people were or could have been wearing. The compulsion had arisen, strangely enough, only when he'd fixed his sights on the nonrevisable past; in history books, the big transitions happen in the blink of an eye, or flip of a page, Edwardian to Great War, Jazz Age, etc.— yet for each *blink*, Alex felt the urge to dress his subjects according to the fashion dictates of the times. Just listening, I could appreciate how tiresome it must have been. In fact, I was becoming more and more conscious of what we had on ourselves. He: modified Nehru jacket, white T-shirt with black collar (an inverted priest) and partridge-green slacks. I had on a pair of Banana Republic shorts. It surprised me how fast we had moved from awkward reminiscence—forced at first to abridge the gaps—to this frankly untested intimacy, and I remarked again how "at ease" Alex had become with himself, and what a change from childhood. And yet the more we talked, the more things . . . well, leveled out. To counter his apparent complacency, I'd begun to feel . . . I hate to introduce a word as obtrusive as "unease" this soon, but— . . . for one thing, it's no longer possible to ignore the fact that I hadn't forgotten them at all. Alex and Eleanor had been surfing the lower registers of my consciousness for some time. I'd turn on my book feed, and there they were—one of her impassioned readings on a store channel, Alex "amplifying" afterwards, with

Lopate One or Two. It had been an itch I couldn't reach, put into words, didn't know I possessed. Subtly, it influenced what I read and avoided. It *unsettled* me that my apprehensions fell so far beyond language, given that everything Alex was about was words. Because the more I paid attention, the more I felt—for all his evident intelligence, sincerity and lack of humor—Alex was "putting one over" on his listeners . . . or was it himself? *Especially* himself. The person on whom this registered most visibly was Eleanor. His sister, the sole reader of his work and constant public companion. Per their "division of labor," she'd decline the inevitable follow-up interview, and if addressed anyway, would say she had "nothing to add." Nothing to add. Oh! Then sit stone-faced, very still, her eyes following whoever spoke, her expression illegible . . . unless you'd known her from childhood. For me those eyes were inexhaustible—I read different things at different times. As he spoke—just now, as we toasted and drank, it was about a roman à clef with mix-and-match wardrobes, dressing the fictional counterparts of friends in V-necks and flared corduroys that, off the page, they'd never be caught dead in—I read in them the old disdain, reaching back to our childhood. She had her own set of dark rings now, just like his. She seemed worn through, in fact—as if all this writing talk was eating her insides away, carping on her like a tumor. This impression was most visible—*unpalatable*—right after she'd read ... —but why? Was it the prospect of having to watch her brother make a fool of himself (as the other part of her expression seemed to imply) in the follow-up interview? He had a spiel he repeated, more or less, regardless of what questions were asked. He'd explain how they split "the work." He performed the "writing part," while Eleanor would read it back to him. By listening, Alex was able to figure out where he'd gone wrong. Sometimes she might make a suggestion—typically of a practical, nonliterary nature —suggestions he never took, he would explain, since he was striving to give her a major yet *mysterious* role in the creative process. Was there any truth to their atrocious charade? Sometimes it seemed to be his doing. Getting back at Eleanor for the insults, betrayals and slights (real and invented) of their childhood. At other times that seemed impossible. The scenario was obviously her devising. It possessed the same clumsiness, flashes of brilliance, the careless falseness of her childhood portraits of an adult world we had yet to be invited into. It also situated her back in her favorite role of victim, no, not victim—the one imposed upon. Straight Girl. No doubt the truth lies somewhere in between—a private joke or world, shared to the exclusion of everybody else, each of them hiding behind the other, taking turns. Our scotch was sinking fast. I'd had two faux-snifters to Alex's three to Eleanor's one. He dominated the conversation, although I made a number of smart-seeming remarks as well. Once Eleanor chimed in with "He's got you there," to Alex, and I turned and smiled at her. She shrugged. So what. So beautiful she could take your breath away. That's what. Dawn was lurking around the corner. The Clynelish, its *resolute integrity, consistent quality, and exemplary strength of character* ballyhooed on the bottle, made the three of us seem lacking by comparison, not decent or intriguing, precocious or demure, as we believed, but *soulless*. So we finished the bottle in exact thirds, chinking glasses for this last round, letting the whiskey diffuse its character into ours. For him, a nonsensical effusiveness. "To improving our hygiene!" he toasted. "To good old B—, more gray days than any other county! The epicenter of crappy yard sales and garden kobolds!" This was so like him. Kobolds. Why couldn't he just say "gnomes"? For Eleanor, a sudden interest in *me*. She asked whether I was surprised to see them. "Of course," I said, blushing, as I took off my blue cap. She wore a white panama hat she didn't remove or fiddle with, and a blue T-shirt with the word MY followed by a pictograph of a bunny. The levels of meta-irony didn't interfere with its inherent sexiness one bit. And she had jeans on. "But—somehow—I can't explain—I *knew* you were coming. Rather, I knew something big was on its way. There were all these signs, and though I didn't know of what, they were coming on fast, *ripening* into reality. Consciously, I didn't know what. But—unconsciously—well, hm—so while I was surprised and of course very glad to see you, I was also pleased with my own powers of projection. See? I said you wouldn't understand." But Alex understood perfectly, or claimed to. Himself, he divided the world into retroactive versus proactive types, and just by the names he chose, I could tell what he thought about each category. You can go around retrospectively assigning portents to every important thing that happens, he said ("and by 'you,' I mean 'one'"), constantly fooling yourself, misreading what's to come, only remembering the portents that turn out to be significant, or you can trace the future's fingerprints merely by *retraining* your unconscious habits, and this time "you" did mean "me." I pointed out the fallacy, which wasn't solipsism but the older one of anticipating the conclusion within the premise, and felt like I'd arrived, somehow, or come full circle, arguing metaphysics with Alex G— . . .

Travel always holds an element of diminution for me— the vanishing of whatever's left behind, the hectic replacement of horizons en route, the disappointment inevitable upon arrival. Train travel works this charm best, or I should say—the *least.* It's the first lesson in perspective, tying parallel tracks to a point signifying infinity, and that spirit, its malicious geometry, adheres to every landscape we ride past . . . traveling backwards is no problem for me, I told them, as we took our seats on the Metro North, tossing my overnight bag onto the rack overhead. They had nothing with them; Alex said they'd sent theirs on ahead, and I said, "How odd," and he agreed, as the train bumped out of its mooring and proceeded into the darkness of the tunnel without announcement. The train was a long time underground. When it emerged from the tunnel, I watched the scorched pillars manifestly the exit grow smaller, its mouth adorned with ivy. Public housing lost out to à la carte high-rises, then brownstones and the backs of stores. The Hudson drew nearer, until there were cliffs on either side. I pointed to some leaves beginning to turn. "Wait till we're in the Catskills," Alex said gloomily. As if all this hadn't been his idea. I put my forehead to the glass and gazed at the rackethead inlets, the ruins overrunning their margin islands, pleasure crafts adrift on the calm sweep of the river, broadening until it engulfed the horizon—I slept for a while, lulled by the slack pull and rhythm of the train. We were picked up at Beacon; I was surprised by the shabbiness of the vehicle, and even more surprised when asked to climb into the back, because the seats were filled with groceries. I wanted to protest. "You won't care," Eleanor said. "Weren't you just reminding us how good you were at fitting into crawl spaces? Remember?" The ride to the Liberty Fishkill & Hunting Lodge was brief, mercifully, but when I got out of the car, it felt like I'd left my grown-up self behind. For one thing, I had to jump down from the bumper, and the man who opened the door leaned over me, nearly double my height. "My god!" I said. There were oaks as tall as redwoods, birch trees as tall as oaks. "Neat?" Eleanor said to me, as I stared at her and

Alex, who was looking more than a little scared himself. "Yes, don't worry," he said, his nose twitching, "we're experiencing the same perspective changes as you." He began to sneeze. "What about them?" I asked. "You'll see," she said. "Alex—don't tell him anything." "Ifbederdadway," he said stuffily. "Better—how?" "More filling." "You'll see," she said. "It's like those Mystery Spots!" I said. "Oh no," she said, suddenly furious, "it's the real deal!" "Well, it's more convincing," I said, "I'll give it that." "Don't be an idiot," she said. Liberty Lodge took the shape of a Swiss chalet and then confounded it with annexes, impediments, steps, sheds, and bowers, the whole semi-serpentine shebang drafted in native pine, the white wood stained darker. The "clearing" it inhabited was encroached by forest on all sides, with barely any room for flowerbeds on the wraparound drive and pittance of lawn several deer were helping crop. Rather inexplicably for a hunting lodge, I thought, but this was made clear later: the deer had come to realize the lawn was the only place where they *wouldn't* be shot at. A woman in a hand-knit shawl approached us from an alcove or door that seemed to open like a cupboard. "I knew you'd be back," she said flatly. "Ms. Barrows, this is Paul," Eleanor replied. "Of course it is," said Sadie Barrows, "and you've brought others. I knew you'd be back. It's always the *curious* ones." "Don't look at me," Alex sniffed unhappily. "It's Eleanor's doing. I hate it here. Oh, god!" "You can't fool me," Mrs. Barrows said. "I've seen you on TV. Get off—I know about the pair of you, acting like you was in the *majors*—" "Excuse me," I said, shocked by everything—but mainly by her rudeness— "what does this ... ?" Eleanor shut me up with a fast look, like she wanted to bite my nose. Once we had privacy, safely ensconced in our cabin, she went over the basic terminology: "Didn't you review the brochure?" No. But I did notice she'd taken the top bunk, Alex the bottom, and I got the cot, how funny was that. Also, I noticed the mess they'd made unpacking, mismatched articles strewn all over, clean sorted with dirty, and so on. *We* were the "minors," Eleanor explained, according to our height—there was a "measuring tree" out in the yard she'd show me in a second, if I'd be patient—and that meant many Lodge recreations and accommodations were off-limits to us, including its main manor's second floor. "*Particularly* the second floor," said Alex. She ignored him. The staff would remain uniformly hostile, "like Surly Sadie," she warned me, except for Franklin the gardener, who was friendly—but not in a

good way. They were known invariably as "mediums."
"Wait," she held up her hand, "you'll have to figure that
one out for yourself." "In good time," said Alex. I put his
new habit of underlining things down to nervousness;
with Eleanor, it was closer to exhilaration ... although
definitely edged with fear. The cabin had many modern
amenities, but its boards were thin and alive to the
moods and weather of the surrounding woods. I went to
the TV and turned it on, the way one does in motel
rooms, but got nothing. There hadn't been any signal
since the multistate blackout, she explained. But that
was over a month ago, I said—but—*again!*—why protest? I decided to adopt a *go figure* attitude to everything
I encountered from that point on. I kept a diary of my
time there, I don't know why—I thought it might be important. We took part in the activities customized for
our minority: hunting birds and small game; swimming, paddle-boating and fishing in the turmoil-colored
lake; rock-climbing and rappelling; sliding down the
zip-line beneath a canopy just coming into autumn
flame, the maples' erratic jennies arrested by our wake
as they spun down to and then below us. I got used to the
new *sequelae* in perspective—the system by which I was
re-*relativized*, so to speak—but the divisions still caused

offense. This was Eleanor's doing, in part; certainly, she harped on its "unfairness" often enough. The signboard on the tripod set before the Lodge's main staircase announced a new entertainment every evening—fun and games we were effectively barred from, since they were held in the Rainbow Room, the Liberty Salon, the Fishkill Bar & Grill, the Roscoe Casino or the Washington Irving Reading Den, all located on the second floor. Of course. That sign was the first thing you'd note upon entering the lobby. A taunt? And the way it stood directly in front of the broad approach to the stairs. A sign—but also a *wicket*. "Nope," said Franklin, "can't do it. There's no sense begging me. You can't go up until you're yay big. I can apologize till I'm blue in the face, but I can't change the rules." "I'm not asking you to change the rules," Eleanor said, "I'm asking you to ignore them, or one of them—just this once." "Nope . . . can't do that either." I couldn't see how they fit so many rooms up there, and said so aloud—but without provoking the response I'd wanted—news of a back annex and staircase. Alex explained instead. Having already defied the stated laws of perspective, we saw things at a distance or high in the air as bigger—or at least *wider* than expected. The science didn't concern me. What mattered was that we were second-class citizens as far as the Lodge owners were concerned. The upper stories were reserved for the last of the basic terms Eleanor had told me about on my first day there, the "majors." This term had very strict usage factors. I never saw anybody described as "a major." On the other hand, he or she might "have reached" or "be in his (or her) majority," under a premise that adumbrated both height and the adult state, if not exclusively. For one thing, they were all invalids ... of a related type. "Why do they look like they're in shock?" I asked. "Listen to him," sneezed Alex. "Why? What did I say?" "Oh for god's sake," Alex said heatedly. "I don't know what your problem is," Eleanor said to Alex, then to me—"if what he claims is so, there's nothing we can do anyway, we're just postponing the inevitable. We won't stay minors forever!" I've recorded her accurately, for what it's worth; notice her correct employment of the term "minors," which she also could have applied, equally accurately, to an individual like me or her brother. With "majors," it's the opposite—it applies only in the present tense and the plural, as with competitive sports and other associations (I can't think of very many) of being *in league*. "We can *leave!*" he screamed. "I don't *want* to leave!" she yelled back. I interjected, but the argument had heated past words into the more fluid contours of will. Hers overwhelmed his of course, both of ours, although I didn't understand fully. How could I? The rude staff admonished ("there are *majors* around!") and separated us. Something terrible had happened to them, no doubt about it, those who'd earned or come up against their majority, and their presence at the lodge (the similarities of affliction and symptoms) was part of their ongoing recovery from whatever frightening insufficiency they'd suffered. I use "insufficiency" because, at that time, I lacked any ideas as to the nature of their ordeal. I use "frightening" because of the expressions on even the stillest features. Unlike Alex, however, I saw no reason to see their fate as inevitable— even if we did stay within the confines of the Lodge—or connected in any way to the second floor. The opposite, in fact, and I explained why. "That would all be well and good if you ever saw one of them go up there," Alex argued. "I've seen them come down often enough," I said, "or being taken—" "Exactly!" he yelled and then sneezed all over his bare hands, starting another fight. We argued all the time. We were constantly being split up by the mediums, who preened themselves on "mediating," and threatened with solitary cabins. "I wouldn't mind one bit!" Eleanor yelled, although I had reason to believe she cared most. Unlike me, she was no Walden lover. I found I got on quite well on my own. I looked at the levels rising and falling on the tree that set daily minimum heights, a Dutch elm that had miraculously escaped the seaboard's mysterious blight—a survivor with a mast that went up thirty feet at least, before any talk of branches began. Sunlight through its leaves stained the unvarnished woodland floor. Today's height was sixteen, the stripe of white paint outside my perspective no matter how far I craned my neck. It was infuriating, no doubt, no matter how I looked at it, it was infuriating. This fielding of one "insult" on top of another (the term was no more than a gesture, a "term of art") was truly grotesque ... I understood Alex—how easy it was to let this place get one down, *feel* the wrongness—a kind of gnawing at the timbers all about us—and establish a set of barriers, bright as sin, simply out of fear, when the reality was always too ambiguous for that. Tomorrow the level could sink down to twelve, or rise to eighteen. Eleanor had a premonition about this number—not the number itself, but how it was figured, which had to do with the numbers in the majority retrieved from the second floor. Serious droughts (like our present one) could make the heights rise to sixteen feet. Improbable, but I had seen invalids *at least* that tall. Of course. We all had. Not tall like real people tall—but more stretched out, I should say, like a normal-sized person if he or she had had his or her molecules rearranged for major-league heights. Incapable of moving on their own but with the easy plasticity of Ken or Barbie dolls: these were the newbies—those newly "brought down" from above. Nights I lay awake listening to the rise and fall of Eleanor's breath, convinced she was as alert as myself and the snuffling Alex, my own breathing attempting to follow in her footsteps, so to speak, and suffocating on my own intake, frightened only of what she might discover. That's not true—but that was the hell of it. The next day we'd be at a different level—the heights and horizons, the trees above us—like the landscape had been swallowed by a kind of river, except it didn't feel cleansing. It rained the whole afternoon, and we were confined to our cabins, more or less, with the main options to read or sleep. As she went from one to the other, Eleanor's breathing became adenoidal and increasingly ordinary. Exchanging glances, Alex and I escaped for a soak. Only a minority of hot tubs were open to us. No surprise; and we didn't mind so much, given the temperatures posted for the majority. Up to 145 degrees, which Alex claimed could peel the flesh right off a person. A normal person. "Go figure," I said. "Go figure," he mimicked, "what are you, her oldest and dearest sock puppet?" We slipped into the scintillating 105-degree scald of the tub known as Newton's Basket in an argumentative frame of mind, and I failed to notice the two people undoubtedly in their majority although only slightly taller than Alex and me, a couple, as they appeared to be holding hands—possibly, intertwining legs—beneath the water level, which, when we'd seated ourselves, reached up to our shoulders or necks. The surprise of them and shock of the heat established a new level inside me. I felt faint. "I don't want to talk," I said to Alex— but really announcing it to them as well—"is that okay?" "Oh, what a shame!" said the woman, while her partner said, "You *sure* you're all right?" at the exact same time. They introduced themselves. They were leaving the lodge the next day—back to "the outside world"—and had wanted to spend their last night in the tub. "To be perfectly honest," Brett said, "we were hoping to run into somebody like you, you know, folks we could practice on . . . we've been so removed from normal life." The Taylors of Cupertino. "Been here long?"

Alex asked. "It feels like ages," Brett said, and Gertrud began to weep, to Alex's and my growing consternation. Me, because I knew how it would go already. I would say and he would say, nourishing more tears on her part, burying her head in his shoulders—and then we'd be treated to a certain display of sorrowful lewdness—her biting him to draw blood was only the most likely item on the shopping list—while Brett carried on his half of the conversation as though Alex and I were witnessing none of this—*nothing!* "Well, you see," said Brett, apologizing at last, "you'd weep, too, if you were in our shoes—if your *shoes* contained multitudes." His shoulder stopped occupying Gertrud, who started to weep again, as if in syncopation with Brett's remarkable sentiment, whether remembering the beauty of it or the ordeal I wasn't able to guess, but whichever it was, the tears suggested they'd come to terms, in a manner of speaking. Lightning deflected in the clouds above our social whirlpool, like beacons or spotlights—nor could we hear the concussions. I would say and he would say and Alex would say and I would apologize immediately and he would apologize as well and Alex would say and I would say, while we agonized over our true meanings, their remembrances, as a fresh round of lightning hit the clouds, and Gertrud, in a rare moment of self-aware-ness, as it had begun to rain, we excused ourselves, only a few drops but still—from that height!—spattered and were able to bring down their targets—some more leaves—mimed the crawl, weeping so, it was hard to re-linquish tomorrow's promise in the rise and fall of the majority's levels, or the day after, fluttering to where I stood, just barely, in the dark. Eleanor was furious at be-ing abandoned—oh, in rare form. For the last time, I no-ticed what she had on. A brown tank top, with calico frills around the V-neck collar and the waist. Flared cords spaghetti-cut below her knees. It worked, given her mood. I finally came out and said it. "You brought me here because you want somebody to go up there with you?" "That's right," she said. "*He's* too afraid." "I follow my instincts," Alex said, shaking like a leaf. "Why not?" I said to her. "You don't know what you're saying," he said to me. "Sure I do," I said, "and I'm surprised you'd let your sister go there without you." He began to curse me, using the worst language he could think of. It was pretty inventive, which led me to believe he wasn't all *that* dev-astated. Once she'd openly admitted what she wanted, and once I'd agreed to this folly or inspiration—frankly, I didn't care either way, a mistake could be more valuable, I thought—there was no point wasting time. We decided the Pushover would work well enough to get past the guard, with our roles (*pusher* or *bench*) to be determined by the sex of the medium. We knew we had to work fast. Larry from catering was on—I let Eleanor handle the talk, miming the crawl behind him on my hands and knees. We went fast once he was down, screaming about his back, but the stairs were more exercise than we'd reckoned, and I hadn't reckoned much. Below the banisters, a lattice-work of white pine, same as everything else, the grille carved with flowery curlicues and windblown hats—I could see the flames of the lobby's hearth through the slits, telescoping its warm invitation. The hapless heads of animals shot in the nearby hills—some snarling, others contemplative. Century-old farm implements reworked into children's toys—their paint aged like a fine wine. The chipped lead in the chandelier when we reached the top. By now there was nobody to stop us, and the first room that presented itself naturally aroused our curiosity. It wasn't much. In fact, it was identical to just about every crummy motel room I'd ever found myself in—in itself, this was more inconceivable than anything we could have dreamt up. This was what we'd been warned off?

Suicidally feared and craved? Eleanor pulled aside the curtains to confirm that we were on the right floor, while I turned on a lamp on the night table separating king- and queen-sized beds. Supporting the lamps was a gunmetal box bolted to the wall, with the purpose, MAGIC WAGERS, written in red caps, and a turret slot taking quarters. Two per bed for five minutes it seemed. On Eleanor's command, I felt in my pocket for change. When they both began vibrating, we laughed and jumped aboard. The mattresses were made and surprisingly soft. "It's like featherbeds!" Eleanor said, and then she screamed, "Agh, a foot!—a hand!" I thought she was being funny, but then I understood. Next to my foot was another foot, and another next to that—and below. And likewise with each hand. Petrified, I realized the essence of what I was lying on. Did horror render me helpless? Which did I lose first? The capacity to move? Or the will? Whichever it was, I realized I had been wrong before, it wasn't as if they had adapted or even succumbed. The word for what those coming into their majority became contained its own language. And yet, even as I merged into the souls or bodies sharing the bed with me, folded in origami-fashion, I never lost the capacity (or the will) for continuous thought: it was like I was flypaper to them, like they were for me, my shock lasting the full contraction of a beat, which passed through these beings without actually disturbing the design of their lasting object worship . . . nor could you blame them—well, *us!*—exactly. Table, lamp, chair. Capgun. Lattice grille. For now these things were our only hope of getting "unstuck."

SEVEN CLUES

"Most heads are routine," he says. "Set the attachment at one of eight lengths, then slide the clipper up the back stretch, cruising from base to crown. The trick to it is there's no trick to it. *Confidence*, son! If coffee's making your hands shake, stop drinking the stuff. How can the customer trust you if your hands tremble all the time? See, one of the things you're doing, you're *reassuring* him ... laying to rest any second thoughts he might be having about coming in, in the first place."

It wasn't a week, and Ward had already had it up to here with his talkative mentor, Frank Reed aka Frank the Barber, in particular his habit of calling Ward *son* whenever he wasn't using "Billy."

"Why? Who knows why? Men are complicated creatures. He figures he wants change and fears it at the same time."

As a matter of fact, the customer was looking askance at the chair Frank had tilted back for him, the barber's prawn-shaped torso tipped over it in a white smock, his expression smoothed through years of surreptitious practice in the wall-length mirror opposite, with the disinfectant drying on his scissors—fresh from the pickle jar.

"Everything you need to know can be learned from the shape of the head, from the parts to the patterns of the hair across it. Look. Here, here, and here. These are yours. The preferences of the patron come in second—a *distant* second. This is where every one of you kids goes wrong at first … by actually *listening* to their preferences. See this customer? What do you think he asked for when he first came to me, when was it? Six years ago? How can a layman judge what's right for his own head? Do *you* trust what you see in a mirror? 'A Dreyfus?' I told Larry—go ahead, tell Billy, Larry, didn't I say that? Exactly? 'With those ears,' I told him straight, 'not a chance! Try the Soviet Bachelor instead.' And you can see how well that's worked for *both* of us—because once I've found the right haircut for one of these fellas—once they see it grown out after, what—*three weeks*?—they'll be back. They'll be asking for the same exact haircut their whole lives, with only minor corrections for age and balding patterns. And if they ever do leave the

County—*ha!*—they'll remember me and never feel as settled into their haircuts of the future. Never. That's the stature you could look forward to one day, son—I'm not saying you will, but it's something to aim for. Now this unfortunate gentleman—" he spread his hand out on top of the next customer's mixed-bag crown, turning the head just a hair so that the man faced Ward with a starved, sour look—"hair's way too fine for a Newman— to get a real Newman, it needs to start curling in at least three-quarters of an inch. Witch hazel should produce results in less than three months. An old barber's trick. A natural or a line? There *is* no hairline on this particular neck. See? The hair from the back keeps going. Brush it back. That broad of a forehead cries out for a widow's peak. But however you choose, stick to your decision, even over objections. Talking is fine. Learn to develop a spiel. Well-crafted banter will set most men at ease. But if the customer isn't talking back, can it. And if the talking affects your judgment, or your style with these old buzz-clippers, then—I think we can all agree—a friendly silence is best."

"You'll need to be careful with the small machinery of those heads. Ordinary people imagine them round, but any half-decent barber knows that the human skull consists of numerous slightly concave, scale-shaped planes touching and sometimes overlapping. The phrenologists of the nineteenth century had the right idea, only they got the names wrong. Lododox! Symbol of the short-fused. How do you like that?"

The fourth customer was a tall black man, but while Frank didn't take the same easy liberties he did with the white ones—the borderline unprofessional violations and manipulations of their space—he didn't allow the customer to interrupt his spiel or influence its direction either. The man was a source of ugly fascination to Ward. He was tall and very thin, and well dressed in a sense—*formally* dressed, but in a cheap suit-and-tie affair that looked and smelled like it had been worn for days, even *slept* in, right down to the damp pinkish-white shirt with the gaudy lapel—to the underwear, no doubt. He stood very erect—established himself in the chair as if *he* were the hinged and lever-ready thing—but erect in a way that was the opposite of dignified, like somebody poking his middle finger into your third eye. How could you live and let live like that?

"Listen up, son. Potent depressives, the Jonahs of the world, reveal themselves by the circumferences of their *misericordia* pumps, near the left nodule of corti. Always listen to your fingers. Begin at the back, always with the back left corner. Left side, right side, top, bangs. Break up the order if you get bored . . . but always take the bottom left first. And make sure the bangs go last. See, it's all about putting things into proportion . . . like the answer to whatever's eating you, you got to do the calculations first."

He'd been a high-school superstar: in the same league as superstars, at any rate. Instead, life surprised Ward with this fuming, hapless, heavy flesh, for which nothing had worked out—disappointment in duds, cowboy hat and overpressed size-45 denim.

"Yep, you're a big one," said Frank Reed, as he met his charge at the bus stop. He leaned over and opened the wagon's passenger door. "Swell, swell. Just put your stuff in the back. So good to see you. Let's take a gander with that thing off you. What do you say?"

Frank Reed had to work to keep his smile from skipping town. Its welcome so wide he could smell his own teeth. The thing attached to the boy's head was a Red Rock West incarnation of Elton John, shaved military-short on both sides with the panel of center-flipped hair, very girlish, running down the back of Ward's thick, sweaty neck.

Both of them felt constrained by the other cars on the Parkway, Frank still reeling from his encounter with a Midwest mullet in upstate's safe conservatory. But he girded himself for the mentoring role he'd requested. And when Ward began to classify the different lowlifes he'd encountered in the institution he'd been calling home, Frank was able to reply, "I can take you back right now, if you like," without skipping a beat. "If you can't learn to talk like a normal person." The boy blushed in confusion.

Frank made an impromptu detour to Pat Mitchell's —"best ice cream in the county!" he exclaimed, feeling windy and apologetic.

"You don't mind if I call you Billy?" he asked, as they compared flavors in the cemetery down the street, the brown waters of the Susquehanna bending west to east to south. "There's this song by Petula Clark about a young man with that name. My wife used to love it."

That was how it started: Ward knew why Frank Reed had taken him on. He'd go over the reasons, one by one, taking his own sweet time.

First for the state money, just as Ward had suspected.

Second to get good with the cops (very useful for a barber) by "taking a chance" on a troubled boy who'd been in the system as long as Ward.

Third, he got somebody who'd have to listen to him, day in, day out . . .

Fourth, as intimidating presence: an implicit threat to Frank's "unruly" customers, ridiculous as that sounded.

More like anybody who might disagree while the barber was holding court, five.

The sixth reason would retain its mystery a little while longer.

Ward had no hope as a haircutter (even as a "butcher," he wasn't primitive enough), but Frank did see enormous potential related to reasons four and five.

"People say the word comes from the Scandinavian, *banga*—meaning to hammer, when in fact it's a horse's tail. Cows and horses. It's interesting how often barnyard animals and their backsides put in an appearance. Cowlicks, ducktails, pigtails, bangs, ponytails. The

list goes on. Words, like hairs, can have interesting der-
ivations. You'd be surprised how many start with
something womanish. Speaking of which—avoid the
straight line across no matter how tempting. It's fine for
young ladies, but you'll lose more regulars with that
than any other—find the natural part and comb it out
at least six times—one, two, three, up to six, in fast
sweeps."

The shop was a modest affair, a discrete door-and-
half-window storefront with no awning facing the
Vestal Plaza's back lot. The only Plaza business that did
face this direction, in fact. Behind the lot, the hillside
created an enormous amphitheater, its upper slope
scalped to an ugly scree. Club House Road circuited it,
winding up to the Jewish Community Center, where the
children of Harpur's professors would learn the language that unlocked the secrets of the original Testa-
ment. Many had become Frank's regular clients, he
claimed. He loved kids, loved getting at people's heads,
knowing their strands as early as possible. Shady colon-
nades alternated with square planters open to the sun—
ficus, fern, American Smoketree under arbitrary pockets of light. Frank had the idea of placing torpedo-sized
barber poles strategically along the Plaza's pitchfork of

galleries, with two near the pizza parlor painted with Venetian gondolas from the life, directing one to a blind alley then out to the parking lot's amphitheater. The same number of cars (more or less) huddled into the same small quadrant in the lot's wide acreage, directly in front of Frank's shop. Every seat in what Frank Reed dubbed his "worker's paradise" filled with impatient, unhappy men.

"If he's keeping them long, try squirting mist on the forelocks. To do it right, you'll want to keep the part as thin as a razor blade. Look at Burt's circa *Hustle* or the very early Alda—the half-ear with sideburns and the long hair part company. Many people have more than one part, of course. The average is three for men. With a little bit of coaxing and a dab of grippy or holding gel, they can be set into even layers no matter how he chooses to part it as it starts growing back—although there are deviations you can't fix. There was this one guy—a two-monther—who had eighteen separate cowlicks, wings and swirls total. Claimed he'd had a great head of hair up until his mid-twenties, when he was diagnosed with testicular cancer, and when the hair grew back, it got messed up somehow. Remember that, Sam? Good-luck Chuck. But no matter how cockeyed things look—there's always the one dominant part. Work the top layer out with a mind to the two ears. Are they level? Because most ears aren't. Typically, the left or right lifts a few milli- or even centimeters higher, corresponding to what-handed you are. Everything's connected—like in that embarrassing Candy Mitchum song my wife used to listen to, a watch ticks, a man dies, the thatch, the taper, how it hangs around the ears, the bangs, the length all over."

Ward unlocked the mystery reason the one time he went up with the old man on a Ferris wheel.

Fear was the key.

The amusement park had been set up in Johnson City to celebrate the latest revelation in indoor shopping, the Oakdale Mall. "This year's pet rock," the barber predicted, but he took his mentee with him to check it out.

The trip turned very frightening when they got trapped at the top. The bar swung down across their laps. The gondola tipped back with the weight of the two of them. Ward, who was taking up more than his share of the seat, was squeezing the metal, his knuckles white, and as the enormous axle began to turn, his terror began to communicate itself to his hapless mentor, hair by hair, by slow but lethal osmosis. Their feet swept out into space, over the hearthstones of the valley.

They were lifted and pulled backwards, above the salaaming green and the dirty dishwater of the pilot lake. There were the different colored lights of the arcades, with the lights of pit stops and parkways and various cartons of industry shoved off to the side.

As his terror grew, Ward suddenly realized that Frank Reed was still talking. Over the dismay of his surprise, he realized this guy was talking because he *had* to. He was afraid of what would happen when he stopped.

"This is one time you'll have to use the mirror," Frank Reed was advising him, "but don't let them catch you! And pray—whenever you're sneaking a look—you don't lock glances by accident. There's the boredom. Of course there's boredom. Years of dead time and grinding molars—times when your customer's behavior or personal odor is so bad you want to clip the nub off the bottom of his ear."

"It's about proportion, balance, cause, effect. Soon enough you'll get so the figuring is sure and automatic. See? Three snips. For thatching, use the first and middle fingers to lever out the locks, then start snipping from left to right, unless you're working with a Jew or Italian, in which case backwards is okay, I guess. Italian cutters are the showiest—but for true masters you'll want to watch the Poles. There was a Lou Dembrowski—a magical Pole I learned from in secret, many years back. He had this talent for *disrupting* the part. But even he couldn't compete with a blowfly cowlick. Now don't cut across the entire wedge. Leave about an eighth of an inch, to hold your place. Comb it out three times when you're finished—forwards, backwards and forwards again. By this point, you should be done.

"No surprises. And no more than five more strokes with your instruments. Two is okay. No strokes is best. End with a brace of tonic, tap on some powder, slap the cuff with a clean towel, hold up the hand mirror. *Voilà!* Sure—it's okay to say it. The big moment. Watch in the wall-wide mirror as the expression changes. Delight? Disappointment? Fair shape? Or a slander? Those who cut hair for a living are lucky. On a busy day, we get dozens of defining moments. 'What would my father say if he could see me now?' In how many professions do you find a man handed that question on a routine basis? Truth or failure sits there in front of you, in the round. And then it walks out into the world. Appearances count—first impressions the most. As my old teacher used to tell me over and over again, there are seven clues to a man's character, all as plain as the nose on his face—choose any stranger. His haircut. His handshake. The shiftiness of his eyes. The clothes he wears. The presence or absence of dirt under his nails. The nose on his face. His smell."

NO SUBSTITUTIONS

Engineered? Nothing doing! Working through the latest batch of arguments in favor of the so-called wind-leasing tax from District Attorney Thornbird's office—washers sponging up the messy linotype—it suddenly struck Conrad Wade: *he had cancer*. It wasn't intuition—Conrad wasn't blessed with anything resembling an "intuitive" sense—so much as putting two and two together, or three and three—however many nagging upsets to his daily flux and flow it had taken to come to this life-altering—*literally*—conclusion: was it too late already? He feared yes. The timing couldn't have been worse. The week before, Conrad had been promoted to Manager of the Photocopies Lab. It was more about the honor than the raise per se, the partners told him—well, not the partners, but their credible agents—his immediate supervisor, Barbara Crandall, Administrative Supervisor Title IV, and her boss one level up, Tony Holloway, a Title III Supervisor, who couldn't or wouldn't bring himself to look Conrad in the eyes. He let Barbara do the talking. Sat with his chair swiveled to the side—his legs splayed out. High-handed prick, Conrad thought, wishing he'd lose his balance—and "whore" flashed through his mind, listening to Barbara explain to him the honor being bestowed, despite the fact she was a grandmother of six—a corpulent, near-sighted martinet on some endless fault-finding mission of her own choosing. *What's wrong with me?* he thought (once the spasm had passed) and looked with horror at the glass of water resting on the table in front of him. "So what do you say?" asked Holloway, interrupting Crandall. "Can I take the night to think about it?" Holloway looked at Barbara—then back at Conrad. "I don't understand," he said. "Are you an idiot? What's there to think about? What was Barb just telling you?" Under the weight of these and similar words—the imperturbable bullying of the Title III Supervisor—Conrad agreed to his surprise promotion and shook both their hands (his comical with sweat). But when he told his roommates, Bob and Chris, it turned out they both agreed with Holloway, upbraiding Conrad for his scruples. "Seriously? You said you'd think about it?" said Bob. "You didn't," added Chris, mercilessly. She was attempting to scrub egg scum from the bottom of a cast-iron kettle—"No wonder he chewed you out." Conrad went over the reasons against: he would be the unpaid monitor of—and informant against—the four Photocopies Assistants who worked alongside him compiling briefs and running the arguments and matters of the week, day or hour (it all depended) across the light-levered windows of the copiers, aligned in banks three deep—handling the entire duplication needs of the district assizes. They scoffed at his concerns. "How old are you now?" Bob said. "Can't you recognize a golden opportunity when you see it? This is your ticket *out* of Photocopies!" "Yeah!" agreed Chris. Bob and Chris were a couple—and Conrad often found cause to resent their patronizing opinions about, or interference in, his personal and work affairs, their acting like common agreement was—a priori, in and of itself—superior to his own judgments and urgent wishes. When they disagreed, however, he liked it that Chris typically sided with him—Bob, she claimed, could be peremptory and narrow in his views. And she disliked his brutal attitudes vis-à-vis sports. He was explaining to Conrad the unofficial license Conrad had been handed to run his own side business—"Think of all the material you could put out there." "I could go to jail," Conrad said—he would also take the heat if any of his new "subordi-nates" (the word made him stumble) were to step out of line, without his knowledge. "Well, keep an eye on them," said Bob. "Yeah," said Chris, "how hard can it be?" Resentment crouched in Conrad's bowels, keeping him awake—a painful, chunky gruel—and terrified by what raced out of him. Visited by intense forebodings and growing rage at his helplessness, in their grasp. Whose—? His head held to a hot iron—not for the first time, he noted. Paper angled from slots, in the rattling copier ranks, while the toothless light cropped back and forth. The taste of glass in his mouth—or blood—maybe the beginnings of another headache. Pages collating on one machine. Another set—one-sided to back-to-front —swayed with a thunk, each time the paper flipped over. Pete Carver—doing three jobs simultaneously be-hind Conrad, on discovery batch 17 for the pool-water poisoning claims around Gramercy Court—inquired what title manager Conrad had reached now, then claimed he had never heard of managers at Title Six, with transparent ill will. Of course he hadn't! Neither had Conrad. Who'd ever heard of a Title Six Manager? It was ridiculous—some upper management joke at Con-rad's expense. And the thing was, he had to keep on eating their foul leavings. The only cure for contact with the beast was cancer—...but by the time a person took note of the "warning signs," it was too late. He knew that much—little—enough. The doctors would quarantine him—maybe murder him outright. He took a calculated risk, and visited the eighteenth-floor clinic on his break. He scooped up *Cancer—The Angry Killer*, together with a half-dozen other brochures, and took them out onto the scorched plaza, where he dumped all but the cancer one into the trash receptacle, and reviewed the symptoms, or tried to ... —a pigeon shat on his one decent suit. Only then did he hear them. "I can connect you with somebody who works at Sam's Club," a woman was saying to her lunch companion. Noon—maybe a bit after—and the sunshine pouring into the interhigh-rise canyon was at full strength, baking and bouncing off the light-colored concrete, boiling—literally—well, not literally—the waters of a receding fountain, fecund with rot. The women lifted the wax around their sandwiches—white bread, a slice of some bologna, mustard, lots of lettuce—and applied themselves to their meal, talking between mouthfuls. "We had a plan—he just never showed up. It was incredible. So after that, I didn't talk to him for three months. Then—last night—he calls me to apologize! Out of the blue. Like everything's totally copacetic. Can you believe that?" "So what happened?" Conrad tried to ignore them. He flipped through the brochure for vectors of transmission—the animal kind included squirrels, raccoons, badgers, skunks, rats, pigeons, and dogs—seemed pretty much *any* animal was susceptible via the humors of blood, lymph, salivary, etc. He read about a new cancer rumor that it could adapt to a mosquito sting—the now "fatal" sting. There were pigeons everywhere—shitting and strutting. Heat and the sunlight were splitting his head open. ". . . back at you and haul off into the unknown—as I said, like, why would I?" "You'd be crazy even to consider it," said the woman who'd been listening. Conrad knew her—Esme—or rather, he'd been introduced once or twice, and then seen her around the Serling—random run-ins and careful smiles (bloodsuckers, the calf-revealing bitches). "Yeah. Of course. But don't you find that weird?" asked the storyteller. Half-listening—it was impossible not to—Conrad had trouble focusing on the symptoms listed in the pamphlet, starting with "abdominal pain"—oh yes!—and proceeding to "anxiety or restlessness that gradually gets worse and may become extreme agitation." The childhood nightmare of self-absorption. Wrung out, but he had to stand—it was minutes past one by his watch. A backward glance took in not only the women but this guy Conrad hadn't noticed before, writing down notes—married, Conrad guessed, or otherwise shackled, no kids, with the spread and stoop of at least fifty years. He remarked Conrad's noticing him with astonishment and then absurd—*gloating!*—satisfaction. The gelatinous leaves of the shrubs shaped, identically, like tiny fans a doll might hold. He went back inside. Of course, the AC was on the fritz. "Where have you been?" Barbara asked. Conrad assumed she meant this rhetorically. He was five minutes late, for crying out loud! The pamphlet was sticking out of his pocket, and he didn't feel up to one of her little chats. Later, he heard her complaining to Emory— "... we show some kindness, take notice and ..."—he could have finished the thought for her—this was what you got. Conrad was removing his copy cap when Emory approached him. There was a current of anxiety about her, he felt, a nervous hate. Fully reciprocated— he thought—when Emory asked whether he would replace the water cooler. "Didn't I do the last one?" Conrad asked. Emory answered, with a question of her own— "Isn't that part of what being manager means?" "What did I ever do to you?" Conrad asked. "What?" "Oh, never mind"—he felt defeated by the creaking futility of trying to argue with them all. In any case, he'd run out of questions. The bottles were stacked in large plastic crates, side by side and on top of one another. The relative density of water to air—the idea that only a hard skin of plastic separated . . . —the compromising of its atmosphere with his, *spilling* onto him, somehow, coming into contact. His fear was out of proportion to the real nature of the threat—he knew this, but could do nothing at all. He remembered another symptom from the pamphlet—"hydrophobia"—and his hands shook as he dragged the heavy tumbler from the crate and balanced it upright. "Well?" somebody said, after he'd stared at it for some time. He was mesmerized by the fear of all that water wanting out. And then he had to peel off the soft tab on top—his jaw clenching at the sight of what was so easily disturbed inside—to lift the cumbersome object, one hand holding it underneath and the other embracing it around the side, the clear fluid pressed up against his face, and tip it just so—so the water poured into the cooling unit and the tumbler upended into the shallow reservoir, without spilling a drop—a large bubble would form, flatten and rise to the top, followed by smaller bubbles and a stir of froth. Of course, it didn't work out this way at all: his front soaked—trousers resenting the wet intrusion, darkness spreading across the material like a thundercloud. Water poured onto the floor, continuing to gurgle from the capsized bottle top, so that Conrad slipped and lost his balance. He was speaking in dialect—making weird sounds Grandma Crandall had never heard her whole long life—arguing all the way to the clinic. The nurse gave him a towel—some towelettes for his scrapes—but otherwise didn't continue examining him, fortunately. She took his blood pressure, however. "What are you doing that for?" Conrad asked. "It's just routine," the nurse said, "what are you so nervous about?" "Me?" "Why do you keep grimacing?" "I don't like parts of me being constricted," Conrad lied. They sent him home early—soaked as he was, he couldn't very well keep making copies of briefs. . . . Chris heard him return—the petulant squish-squish of his shoes. "What happened to you?" she asked, needlessly. She watched as he sat on the floor of the bathroom and peeled off his socks like they were items of skin. When he tried to explain, she reacted glibly ("So what's the problem? We're all two thirds of us water"), which hardly improved his mood. Conrad changed the topic. He talked to Chris about her dog, Olivier, who was still missing, she said, adding to her many worries, and then Bob came in, and Chris caught him up, and he added his own two cents as always, and Chris and him talked about some other things, and then they left. Imagining the two of them fucking, Conrad started to masturbate, but his stomach reacted badly. Tonight's installment was a viscous liquid smelling like the wet hay some corpse had moldered into, etc. "You're talking funny," subgrade-ordinary Jeannie informed him the next morning. "Funny—how?" "Slurring your words," she said. He was handing out the day's copying assignments to her and Carver, Emory and Rawls. His deputies as such. Conrad spat into a vile handkerchief— "That better?" Nobody said anything one way or the other. He hadn't slept a wink—reviewing the pamphlet over and over, trying to memorize the symptoms recorded there, in the correct order. He closed his eyes, and immediately cuntfaced ghouls pursued him into waking—this nightmarish heat wave that refused to break. But the size of the morning sun! Walking to work—across the superheated plazas and palisades set above busy Riverside Drive—morning's honking migration—and overlooking the Chenango East—a little more than a mile to the Serling Building—which he did even when he was fried dark and crispy, and near likely to faint by the time he climbed the stairs to the second floor lab, like today—when at his feet, Conrad suddenly noticed a gentleman's card, on the macadam set ablaze. Their island city was compassed by the Chenango West, the Chenango North, the Chenango East and the Chenango South, and each had become a mirror for the sun to bedazzle itself in. The rivers' light overflowed the city and tormented even as it probed deeper ... even this early in the day. The midtown towers crushed into tinfoil by the heat of the summer sun. Conrad had never felt it hotter. He wiped the sweat from his face and neck—back and front—with a handkerchief that quickly became transparent—*wringable*—with his spoiled seepage. He was near the urban pasturage where 48th Street turned in from the cars lined along the river —an overgrown sewage inlet, or outpost—not near, at. The card was in the middle of the road shared with infrequent traffic, away from the sidewalk's stubbings of trash. Literally heaps of trash—as usual, the neighbors hadn't thought things through. He had a hard time reading it—DEAL OF THE SUMMER became *the dead of summer*— and by the time he grasped its significance, the card had risen two feet in the air—flipping about like something caught in a ventilator updraft, except there was no grating nearby—not even a pothole—. . . nor did it return to the pavement. The "updraft" carried the card past Conrad's astonished face and kept it going, until it had risen out of sight. In retrospect, he would believe he had witnessed—could have walked through—one of the first of their city island's *fame pockets*. Areas of inexplicable atmospheric disturbance originating on a remote side of the globe—they'd been fanning out at a disturbingly rapid pace—to the point where they were popping up throughout the eastern states. And now here. In the flesh, so to speak. He'd seen the tape and barricades thrown up around these antigravity pockets—the black-&-white photos in the *Daily News* and the green, grainy footage on his Singer-issue TV—crowds of idiots holding back from throwing things into the *dead air*, for the sake of fame, posterity, whatever—and he'd heard of their awesome irrationality during bouts of actual weather—ascending water funnels and other sights so awful they couldn't be picked up on tape. According to the latest Donald Bach rumor—the writer-guru whom Chris urged upon Conrad and everybody she could— the antigravity pockets served as transportation chutes that could lift or carry the occupants—*any* object or creature, but only humans, safely—into the space outside our planet's protective ozone. Their mayor labeled the thing a hoax and threatened Bach, as its author—the "master of fictional mayhem"—with a list of lawsuits and damages should he dare set foot on their island city. "Hence all the extra work for us," Conrad apologized to his disgruntled subordinaries—Pete Carver, Emory, Jeannie, Rawls—coming to a conclusion of sorts. He'd made it through! He wiped his face with his handkerchief and heard groans of shock from the group. "You SPAT in that thing!" one of the men yelled at him, very angry. Measured against his morning vision and his upcoming and unavoidable death, their complaints sounded pretty stupid. How could he explain to them what he'd seen? The light surrounding the card had felt different—like copier backwash leaking out the sides of the floppy mat. The thicker the law, the more light escaped—a gangrenish but still yellow halo. He controlled this light—literally—with his fingertips. But what if, for every word he copied, something in the real world had to be erased? Was that the look of it? All of these uninformative back-and-forth arguments. They attacked him in the mouth—the teeth, in particular—first. He feared the light's movements, as it scraped the glass plate's underbelly. The fear of certain forms of repetition, smoothly or not so much, riding back and forth, back and forth—their yellow shadows fly across the ceiling—the physics and electrical chemistry of so much duplicative destruction. Now, in order to breathe, he had to relearn how to salivate—or learn how to resalivate—so that his throat muscles wouldn't seize up due to the disgusting saliva he was forced to swallow—a struggle every time—time and again forced to spit into the contentious handkerchief, or (very discretely) some nearby wastepaper basket. He popped four aspirin against his head splitting apart. He reviewed the next batch of symptoms: "painful sensitivity to light"—that had worsened, obviously—"pain, burning, itching, tingling, or numbness at the site of the bite or original exposure"—he kept searching his hands, feet, legs, arms, shoulders, and middle for this carcinogenic transfer node, always without success—and "paralysis," which didn't frighten him at all (*oh* no—!). He popped six aspirin to cope with his headache. Behind the pain was the grinding anxiety—his constant enemy, which would take over—rule him into ruin—given half a chance. Somehow, he survived his eight hours in the heat made unconscionable by the linoleum and fluoride couplings in Photocopies. It was a laboratory all right. Then, home —all but groping his way beneath the unendurable sun. People always say the end of one thing means the beginning of something new. The fear of *any* change. He walked home the way he'd come that morning— or thought he had—but was unable to locate the *fame pocket*—barely noting his surroundings, so carefully was he scanning for alterations in the battering sunlight, scared of walking into something—dead air or what, he didn't know. Given his stage-four cancer (the most contagious stage), he was feeling life to be all the more precious, even with its many painful impostures, or maybe because of. He was in that kind of mood. He knew he was getting close to the house when he saw Olivier's missing posters stapled into the splintering phone-poles and plywood window-boards. He certainly looked lost in the grainy black-and-white blowup Bob and Chris had chosen, ignoring Conrad's opposite advice. One glance—even proximity—caused an irrational sense of gloom and guilt to settle upon him. He wiped his perspiring face with the unclean handkerchief. "So what if I did?" he thought. His stomach tightened as he felt the justice in avenging himself—ironically, outside the law. Bob was still at work, and Chris was lying on the living-room couch when Conrad entered—immediately stuffing the hankie into his pants pocket—rereading the first book in Bach's "Tweaker's Trilogy," as it was called, *Into the Unknown*, followed by *Left Behind* and the satisfying series coda, *Beyond the Fifth Dimension*—for what, the nth time. These books were her bible. Chris extrapolated her rules for living from their arguments or plots—something that elusive. In short order, argued Bach, this planet would no longer be able to sustain human life, or any other. Those who truly lived without fear, he claimed, could be transported out into space—bubble-wrapped, so to speak, in transparent cryogenic suits capable of infinitely recycling each individual's basic needs—breathing, eating, excreting, receiving data—so that she should never die, unless the suit got torn or the wearer hit, vaporized, pummeled, shot, or set on fire by whatever happened to be out there. For those who held onto the species' final afflatus—their *fear*—the nightmare would be endless: "turning, revolving, drifting from planet to planet, across abysmal stretches of space or time or space-time, insane, alone, frightened, unable to remove yourselves from the suits —or too scared to try." "I saw the posters," Conrad said to Chris. "You know, you guys were right—I think they *will* work!" "I haven't heard a thing," said Chris, sitting up a little—"I'm trying to take my mind off it, you know? Bach is such a creative fuckin' visionary!" she yelled. "What time is this?" "Oh, you know—I've lost count. Deliberately. I mean I think that's a stunted way to go about approaching his work. There's so much there— just think how it's all going to go down! Sorry, no offense, Conrad—I'm really upset about Olivier, you know!" "None taken—all I meant was…" He gave up: "I'm going to lie down." So much had happened already, in the space of a fortnight, Conrad expected things—his symptoms and so forth—to keep accelerating. Instead, to his surprise, he was handed a three-day reprieve—hanging onto the complaints he'd habituated to, with nothing new added—so that he was able to focus his attentions on building a fire-seeking device, splitting the difference between two sets of instructions he'd picked up on the antique-hunter's circuit. He attached the circuit breakers to a simple timer, applying the delicate instruments to the copper wires with a deftness that belied his illness. He followed—and extrapolated from—the neural pathways he saw in the two competing diagrams. Splitting the difference—more or less. Of course, he had no way to test his work. Reprieve or no, it was still three days without real rest. On the morning of the fourth day, things returned to normal: Conrad discovered he was unable to move his left arm or leg. He looked upon them—his whole left side, in fact—with horror: attached to him—more than attached—but nothing left of his meridian seemed to truly *belong*. He tried to think commands, conscious appropriations to make the limbs shift or lift, retract or inch somewhere even a little. The slur of heat across his sweating chest—its sensation just ending, at which point it could as easily have been ... *ice!* So paralysis was next—to remove any remaining doubts. The thought of the device he'd made—the lasting property damage it would inflict—gave him strength. It was just sitting in a shoebox underneath his bed. His final lesson or statement. The paralyzing anxiety—or actual paralysis—passed away otherwise. "Listen," said Bob, as he shook his corn clusters into a bowl and added milk and two packets of Sweet'N Low. "What's the matter with your face?" "What—?" said Conrad, "nothing!" "Suit yourself—but you've got toothpaste, in any case." He pointed to a corner of his own mouth, as though Conrad were some exotic bird that copied everything. "Conrad," Bob said, "it isn't working out. You know that too, right?" "She's mad about the dog." "Can you blame her?" "But Chris is—you're both blaming me! Is that fair?" "It's not just that." He didn't argue—in his condition, what was the point? Bob allowed him two weeks to find somewhere else—they agreed that seemed a reasonable amount of time. Homeless! Last night he'd dreamed of floating through space in a soiled dry-cleaning bag, reliving the earthly arguments of the last month or so, through yet another solitary eternity. The next symptom—"wide fluctuations in temperature, pulse and blood pressure"—followed him to work. He got in before everybody else—and easily deposited the device behind a loose asbestos panel in the northeast corner of the lab. Conrad knew they were too cheap to leave the security cameras on outside regular work hours. Turned out to be perfect timing. He was called into conference with Crandall and Holloway (apposite agents of Conrad's doom) at the start of the workday—she went over various offenses, the ways his work had plummeted since his promotion, until Holloway interrupted. "The point is," he said, "enough's enough—we've taken the liberty of cleaning out your desk for you." In the ensuing hubbub—Conrad taking heed of the fact that he had nothing to live for, nothing to *give* his life for—it wasn't surprising that those who escorted him from the Serling and across the oversized esplanade with its surfeit of dangerous concrete corners—benches, planters, and fountains—a hand on each elbow, would fail to notice—amidst Conrad's gnashing of litanies—the way his saliva was beginning to foam yellow. Nor how he bucked and threw was due as much to spasms as to anything else. Why should they? Their focus was removing him from the premises—he laughed and drooled into his napkin as he walked away, leaving the overturned box where it landed, office supplies and so-called personal items spilling out. "I did it!" he said, thinking of the device, "I actually did it!" He wiped his face with the handkerchief—realized what he'd done—laughed—spat into it. Chris was a slow reader: close to a week had passed, and she was still on page 54 of Bach's introductory volume, *Into the Unknown.* "Jonathon thought about it," she read—"repeating his life, over and over—on to infinity —without remembering, within each life, the identical lives he'd lived before, and would live again—and so on—into the unknown infinite." Once you knew the big revelations, Chris thought to herself, Bach's hectoring digressions made a lot more sense. Like some animal,

Conrad had bit her on the thigh, causing bleeding—he drooled carcinomic suds into the area—spittle flecks flying as his face changed expression with alarming speed. With the blood pounding in her ears, she couldn't hear her own voice—no, she'd lost it! Chris tried to scream. She pushed him off her—he toppled sideways easily, collapsing into a cursing heap—then up and ramshackle out the door. *Cancer!* she thought—and suddenly Olivier and everything since her dog's disappearance became clear as crystal. *Crystal!* Even during the worst of the horror that afternoon, Conrad was sustained by the strength of the day's accomplishments. Not vengeance exactly, or justice—but *fair play.* The pride of reckoning—dismal, devious, desperately short-lived, but still . . . —"I did it!" he said, wiping the liquid that seeped out of him—from every perorating orifice —with his soaked handkerchief, glad the water was escaping, but terrorized by the fact that it still had contact with him, the icing on the cake of his oncoming dissolution and corruption—"I finally did it!" Seizures and partial paralysis couldn't prevent his escape to the Battery Tunnel. Of the many currents available, he chose the one he believed most harmonious. A safeway patrol caught up with him as he scrabbled over the lightning fence—the chain-link sparked and swayed before snapping—and followed him into the sewer system underneath (fashioning shit into fuel), taking potshots while he stumbled and retreated and finally fell in. They stood over him and discussed the miseries of stage-four cancer. With a resigned but steady arm, one of the men put a bullet where it would be learned best, nothing engineered. "At least he's through working," another said, summing up.

TOM THIMBLE

What a simple thing a breeze is, unless you try to make sense of it! Just so, from that critical summer, only the most fragmentary rumors remain ... and yet they seem to come back every decade or so, like bodies hatching out of older bodies, like once-benignant thoughts and other, better, more *cheerful* revisions.

Another day another redundancy to respond to, a new argu-ment for horror ... thinking again about throwing in the towel ...

A bumblebee replaces a caterpillar—a chrysalis is bro-ken—wherever there's evidence of doubt and they are bridled in the syringa, broom, chickweed, clover—resurrected in the yellow petals that stained poor Teresa's hands. She'd been obsessed with Paul ever since grade school. But for reasons she understood but never considered fair, she wound up Keith's girl—Keith, who was Paul's fifth best friend, a gangly hick with a cotton-wool complexion, an aberrant buoyancy, and a thing for speed—vehicular, mostly. She picked the flower apart, ignoring the campus textbook spread level to the grass. She'd slipped four tabs of glory under her tongue, enjoying the fear that accompanied knowing there was no turning back now, that in an hour's time there would be no familiar knowledge, nothing to latch onto. If things worked out. *He loves me—he loves me not.* Imagining the roadmap of possibilities for each—quite an alternative to put down to the number of petals invented for some random weed—Teresa thought about the years she'd spent under his spell, the longing that seemed to belong to the different, better person she was hoping to become. She hated the word "crush." It made it sound so immature and *under*wrought, when the truth was the opposite, her feelings had changed her, jarred her into a maturity she'd felt ill-equipped to handle—still did, to an extent. The hills and meadows around Harpur campus come chock-full with daisies, feeling their way forward, waiting to be plucked, loves requited and unanswered— by the number.

It's a form of autosuggestion—or hypnosis, if you accept the tax on extremes, a tax he levies. He wants to summon back a generic childhood, but isn't able to without dissembling. That's true of everything he attempts, but more true of certain things like childhood. No childhood is ever truly generic, after all. When I was a kid I believed in all sorts of crazy shit. For example, when I was nine, I fell madly in love with M. C. Escher. I had the Taschen Graphic Works with the Möbius waterfalls and the monks in polygons that mocked perspective, I bought the albums with Escher-derived covers and listened to their messages from the country without understanding what they were really about. The silliest one—the one that struck me as silly even then—was the two hands drawing one another. So why does it bother me so much now—?! Like two copulating slugs—composing even the hairs on the back of the wrist. Of course, the answer is obvious. Him. *I mean why it should* happen to me. *I've done things I'm ashamed of, but I'm not a terrible person. At least, I never thought I was until*

I met him and he started convincing, no, nothing so granular as convince, he simply upset my previous notions—but how could he not—? I'd always known about him.

Now that summer's swallowed half the year, the other seasons feel more or less redundant. Its appetites immense—fierce thunderstorms—mists that blanket the entire county, impenetrable but for the leftover lightning twitching now and again, *he loves me—he loves me not.* Teresa had always been Teresa, no contractions. Her mom and dad were too voguish for Tess, Terry or anything else. While she mattered little enough to those who knew her—not to her parents working their way up the bridge-set ladder, or to Paul, not to her best friend Tracy or Keith or anybody, for that matter, in the group she'd gone to Woodwalkers Pond to "trip and strip" with (slipping quietly away at the start and not missed since) —her disappearance, along with the two other young women her age, Genevieve and Adele, was to have the profoundest consequences for the residents of Bearden for generations to come. Unlike the other pair, who'd been reported right after the bacchanal debacle, Teresa's vanishing went undocumented until sixteen hours later, when her steady, Keith, regained enough of his senses to ask about her, neither parent having noticed anything "amiss." They located the aging-wistfully couple on 1240 Burris Road, at the bottom of the Stonehedge Creek tract, James Lansing cinching back the acrid smoke and tossing the cigarette into a puddle at his feet, where it went out with a quick sizzle. He wished his wife would hurry up. He was in a lousy mood, having lost—been swindled out of, he suspected—several hundred dollars by the Dekkers, a husband-wife team of astonishing virtuosity, both in bidding preliminaries and the bluff—the heart of the game, so to speak. The *Evening Press* reported last night as one of the wildest in memory. The beginning of the "era of storms," perhaps. As for the end of the era *they* knew, that's just fact. He was brusque with Stephanie when she came out, finally, after delaying the polite goodnights (by this time it was the following afternoon)—swatting the folded newspaper arrhythmically against his squeaky nylon slacks, the pleasurable buzz from his thirty-seventh very dry martini having been tied into a knot, and the knot secured and tightened against the area of the occipital, mainly.

Conduit . . . intersection of neck with brain. Whereby I suspect he's surreptitiously switched from four corners to five. I remember Vestal's Five Corners very clearly—the many times I'd biked over with my little brother, Reynold—but is it all "prompted" memory, or the future of what—? We rode there whenever we could—whenever we had the dollars and change saved up. Basking beneath the blue whale emblem, our island nirvana—a white, green, and powder-blue pentagon carved out by Front Street to the south, the Vestal Parkway to the northwest and northeast—a sort of roof-shaped boundary—Stage Road to the west, and North Main Street to the east—Carvel's—our favorite relief from the heat, beating even the town library a few blocks down the Parkway, in back of which we'd meet with our peers and establish council with the purpose of lighting off long strings of fireworks—cracklers and cussers and M-80 blanks. For softserve, nothing was better than Carvel's—just like nothing topped Mitchell's for the hard. The petty dust of the Parkway rapidly churned and re-sifted by the tires of the endlessly passing traffic—Five Corners was always busy—seemed to be kept off the lawn by an invisible force field let down when the franchise shuttered for the evening. Oh, the rose colors in Bearden's repertory of sun-

sets that summer! Reynold was still very attached to his ba-
nana-seat bike, while I had graduated to the ten-speed. The
frozen smoothness seemed to hold off the heat of the sun for the
time we attacked with our parched lips and tongues. The
ridiculous—yet kind of frightening—carousel out front. So
where did it come from? I mean all the dust on the roads every
summer. It made for pretty sunsets ... something I'd learn
about later on.

What were they doing in there? he'd muttered, as he went
about lighting another cigarette. It was at this point that
the normally easygoing Detective Inspector Stanley
Madison—who volunteered Sundays to "direct traffic"
at his local place of worship, in Endicott—lost his temper with Lansing. "Good heavens, man, you mean you
felt *nothing at all?* For your *own* daughter? Didn't you
wonder where she'd *been* all night? During the storm of
your and my lifetime?" Her poor dad was in tears, but it
was true—and in the eyes of the law, he was culpable for
it. Not one iota (*not even a peep!*) of premonition. Not an
intuition, even. Madison flipped through the polaroids,
most tinted the sienna of the toilet bowl still rusting

into the mulch of his backyard pen, memorizing her face at different ages, in different attitudes, against the underdefined but typically festive backdrops, as with colored balloons. Somebody was bending over a plate of cutlets. On the back of one badly developed "intimate," she had penciled her initials. Sometimes, thought Madison, it seemed the poor girl's fate affected nobody but *him*! Calling all tall vessels. He tapped the county's willing volunteers—nearly 150 men stood forward, nearly a third who knew the Lansing couple (now cruelly disgraced), whom Madison organized nearly two-thirds of, splitting them into eight search parties. Able Crutchman's was composed of a widow's dozen, and they all appeared in cheerful humor—rather callously, he thought, given their task and what they might find if they, what—*succeeded?*

That's not the question, of course . . . if it were just a matter of his lying about the facts, making up a story, that would be one thing. But the lies infiltrate everything, even the innocent questions, even the sprinkled-in truths. I am powerless to stop him, or not powerless but not enough . . . he frightens me, of course—the name alone.

For the umpteenth time, Frank Reed was relating how scary weather had brought down a commercial prop plane he'd been commuting in, the "unscheduled landing" in a cornfield far outside Bearden borders, down in bitter Pennsylvania, which recalled Larry Helmsford—never to be outdone in the repetition-of-personal-reminiscences department—to the time he and half the town of Gleeck Bends had scoured the fields for wreckage of a DC-7 that had exploded in midair. "I remember there was stuff—fuselage, part of a wing, seats and suitcases—laid huggerdy-muggerdy over close to fifty acres, and that's no exaggeration." "Body parts?" asked Simon Plackard, who fancied himself a realist—he was told to clamp it. Crutchman sighed. They stood in their assigned huddles pondside, waiting to be told which direction to wander off in by Madison or whoever was in charge above him. *What am I doing here?* Crutchman asked himself as he stubbed out another Camel smoked to its tar-soaked filter, his third since arriving. Just east of dawn, he'd followed his fellow townsmen single file through loafing weeds—sleeves, burrs, collars and frills to their hips or waists still loaded with dew—hopping puddles down the hemmed-in cowpath, through a tough brace of bushes to the long row of pines that ceremonially bordered the pond: Woodwalkers, which had only its reputation as a *nudist swimming hole* to recommend it, and where, the night before last, eleven Harpur students—six boys and five girls—had decided "to investigate [. . . *instigate?*] one of Bearden County's famous hauntings." In the acid-enveloped chaos, three of them —all girls, as it happened—had vanished. The others were pretty shook up—shock, exposure. None of the stories matched up, but that didn't mean a damn thing. There wasn't a man in Crutchman's party he knew with any regularity; there were two he'd made a point of avoiding while growing up, and four others who weren't total strangers, but that was it. Their chipper spirits set his teeth on edge. He felt grateful for the approach of a deputy with a mimeographed close-up of the terrain from County Records onto which he'd proposed in magic marker their target dispersals for the morning. "We'll join up here," Deputy Doyle pointed to a bend in Mockingbird Creek, "no later than noon." The lines, circles, and initials resembled an offensive block-and-tackle diagram: *Coach or assistant?* Crutchman, who despised team rituals, wondered.

I'm putting off saying it, but—diagrammatically—the name goes something like this: two small t's which lay together in crux. In general each lane represents one of the four ways open to us at any given moment, according to Bach's theory of the quadruply divided heart (hence the importance of crosses in all kinds of religious and metaphysical iconography) at the heart of an intersection. Some lanes are more intimidating than others, but does that make them wrong? Ethically speaking . . . he comes for us when we aren't looking—when we've turned away, rolled onto our sides, trying to get comfortable—my harbinger of his future—his invidious distortion of mine, ours, *carrying disease and starvation and only one ending—we fear the worst.*

Careless with his water, Crutchman wolfed down his biscuit ration early and, shortly after 10 A.M., found himself in decidedly lousy shape. He'd used up a lot of energy swiping at the mincing haze of mosquitoes around him, which whined as they probed for DEET-free spots, not to mention the nippy blackflies who didn't seem to mind the spray's smell one bit. The area had a mocking aura to it, he'd decided—slovenly meadows through which disguised—deceptively whiskered—ponds were dispersed, the unhygienic remnants of old Glimmerglass Lake, together with pine barrens, their floors littered with disposable tweezers, doorknobs made of spatulas, and filth in weird rust and orange flavors. Water everywhere—but it was all putrid, undrinkable. Subdividing until they got down to pairs who were supposed to remain in sight or clear hailing distance of one another, somehow Crutchman separated from his partner, the worst barber in Bearden, more than separated or even out of range—*lost*—when he stumbled across English Thomas's cabin (the "Woodwalker"), deserted except for the body curled up tight as a fist in the northeast corner. New, old, hard to know—this "gift" was baffling in many respects, but none more so than the nearly total absence of *smell*. It was like an episode in the torture-and-sorcery series he'd picked up recently at the Fat Cat—the shack was *only findable when I was lost*, defeating Crutchman's sincere attempts to retrace his steps and frustrating Inspector Madison for another five hours. And yet the body was still "juicy," Dr. Charles

("Chuck") Otis determined, when he arrived on the scene some time after that. The procedure—blind-folded, he'd been sent spinning into the buggy, scratchy pines—was absurd and surely unnecessary. That is, if you broke the skin, it would bleed and bruise, even though rigor mortis had set in. But there was dust, in layers, compacted like the lint that accumulates in the backs of appliance filters, undisturbed, along with a year's worth of seasonal damage, *at least*, inside the cabin, disturbances everywhere but on the corpse itself, which hadn't been touched by the inquisitive animals. Nor was there evidence of time-complicit decay, natural or artificial preservation, nothing making sense any-way. He was buck-naked save for a sort of football hel-met of the future, a future which very possibly included some kind of *devolution*, with nodes and antennae as fri-able as the pine tweezers outside. The pathologist whis-tled as he worked—not happily but in low astonish-ment at everything he saw—the critical points of confusion, biological paradoxes, multiplying impossi-bilities—facts and aspects that shouldn't have been served in tandem, yet were—intangibly taunting Otis's "professional expertise." "Can you give me a time?" In-spector Madison asked, physically crowding the doctor.

He had a way of doing this. "Can I give you a time?" "An estimate, then." "Well, right now I'd say anywhere between sixteen hours and twenty-five years. Is that helpful?" "No, not very." Crutchman was going over it again with a local press-hound who'd somehow lost his way in, like a moth, enjoying the brief flame of his fame. "I'd been thinking if ever there was a place one could disappear into, this was it, and that got me thinking you know that maybe *I* had disappeared also, and just as I started getting *really* scared, that was when I saw it—the shack was right there in front of me . . . ! Oh god," he said suddenly—"oh god, what's *that*?" A pair of Otis's assistants had been working to remove the helmet of the future, and when they did, a near-perfect encasing of flesh pulled off with it, like a rubber Halloween mask covering the entire head, but thicker, its color and consistency suggesting fishmeal and cheesecake, and, to the untrained eye, blood-free. "Careful," the pathologist said sharply to his terrified assistants, while eyeing the "rupture" with considerable skepticism. "Come on now, *be careful* with it. Unfuckingbelievable, Jesus. In every case—*every* case—this sort of *constant frightening* syndrome can be traced back to one's childhood."

Different childhoods, different strains ... the Watchtower's witnesses have been vindicated after all! Oh, not really, but let's pretend anyway ... different generations, that's it! That's the solution. Beneath the air-freshener's chimerical repining, the place smelled bad, an institutional smell— bleaches trying to corner the decay, medical and elementary waste, with truly strong smells (natural or artificial) attenuated by the constant assault of recycled air. The home was the same—tile and fluorescences overwhelming the frail inhabitants who survived day to day to be rolled into the patterned hallways before their doorjambs, docked to every stroke on the clock it seemed—wherever their carts and chairs' front wheels swiveled them—catatonics and heebiejeebies, paralytics too. "Are you come to take me home?" a scared old woman asked—the refrain carrying a morsel of hope, whence the tragedy. She could labor under her own steam, so to speak, without walker or cane, even though her mind was gone. She was a stranger to Reynold and me ... a complete stranger. She asked twice more and would have followed us, but I was worried she'd frighten my little brother. "No," I said, "we're here to see our grandma." "But I'm your mother!" the old lady

*yelled at us, riled and suddenly incredibly mean. I think of him
like that—a false claimant, who makes his impression last on
noise alone—but his name . . .*

But in the southwest corner of the cabin—a fluke?—the
officials discovered other, better means to identify the
body, first and foremost a spiral-ring gazette, its binder
two-thirds full with an odd assortment of postcards,
notecards, stick 'ems, perforated appendices, normal
and legal-sized paper and pads, some folded down to
eighths, some beyond that—everything written on, in
two noticeably different hands—tied down with an entire roll of black typewriter ribbon, unknotted, just
weaved and staggered through many turns, horizontal
or vertical, with the two tall *t*s the binding made on either side of the gazette, together with a deck of playing
cards missing seven—three in hearts, two in spades, and
one of both clubs and diamonds, all numbers, no aces or
faces. Frank—Crutchman's search "buddy"—had also
turned up, appearing out of nowhere, without blind-
fold, and his lazy eyes goggled when he saw the signs on
the cards. "Give 'em here!" he said. "My my my, that's the

Coleman deck!" In full, it would have comprised four sets of thirteen and the two "place" cards—the jokers—as in a normal deck, but with different emblems on the suit- and face-cards:—a red and bubbling carafe—a diamond-shaped patch of yellow crocuses—a snake curled into a sideways figure 8, jaws open to swallow its tail—a cross with three bars, the lower two crossing (from left to right) at a tilt upwards. Those were the suits. Just so, Madison was able to surmise the identity of the "victim"—somehow a dead body always seemed like a victim to him, a victim of death at the *very* least—without having to pore over a single line of the spiral-ring gazette. Frank—the owner of the barbershop in the rear of Vestal Plaza—collected gossip as part of his livelihood, and passed it along for the price of a haircut or a shave. As a matter of fact, he'd claim it was his talent as a *gossip* that had kept him in business lo these many years. The body inside the face-sucking helmet from the future appeared to belong to one Tom Coleman, son of Sandy and Mike, brother of Tom—yes, another Tom—the Colemen? To understand the connection, Frank Reed explained, you'd have to go back a decade or so, to the year of the 1974 Bearden Time Capsule, and—at the very least—what it portended for our *future creators*.

Wrong! Just as in life we are surrounded by death, so they say . . . torn by hand and by mouth, stabbed and stormed by penknife, balled around gum chewed until it had lost its flavor—all flavor!—coffee and tobacco drool, papers applied like sponges and saucers—pages, tatters, clippings—pamphlets with the staples wrenched free and the contents shuffled or chucked around—liberated indices—recycled stock and appendix, catalog, and perforated computer cards, particolor confetti of till and bonded spaghetti—the exploding device, so to speak, lying badly wrapped and tied with sixteen or some-such turns of black typewriter ribbon, stretched and with most of the carbon stripped off in the fumbling of the cross-and slipknots, but even so, barely containing the interintimated papers, some taped or pasted onto pages but toward the end slipped in wherever they'd fit, lying on the scratched-up surface of the desk, an overstuffed black leather-bound notebook, its cover marked with the initials TT. His name is Tom Thimble . . . his origins loathsome. *To be sure,* EVERYTHING *about him is loathsome, but in the maker's catalog of his loathsomenesses,* origin *may well take top billing. His maker is not to be envisioned, so that's part of it . . . he is in me, yes, but he is in* you *also.*

By the time the Commemoration & Events Committee got its act together and was ready to publicize the contest rules for inclusion in the Bearden Time Capsule—the burial to be performed on July 4, 1974, by Mayor Williams and his Council of 24 with due pomp and allegory in front of the bandstand in the small Town Park at Five Corners—there was a slapdash quality to the whole venture—the typo-filled forms, the scarcely parsable instructions, the ragged, contrary criteria all *pretext* for a selection process that would prove as mystifying as it was hurtful, aiming (it was widely felt) to offend as big a swatch of "practicing" families as possible—violating basic standards of decency and fairness, leading to the ridiculous scandal or butting-of-heads relating to the selection of the Coleman Deck for the capsule. Frank opined how unnecessary it had all been: "They didn't know the difference between *practice* and *practicing*? What can you do with duly elected officers that stupid?" "Unelect 'em." "Stars and feathers," said one ugly customer, quite drunk on horrors, "and then drop them at the border." "*What* borders?" asked Inspector Madison. "Break it up now, you hear?" It was as if the "Cake" Committee had spent all its precious preliminaries in out-fielding and infighting just to *choose* slapdash—impro-visation, *process over form*—as the county's preferred mode of preservation, 100 to 250 years into the future. Stumbling over cryogenic gnomes and pennies, and other such "worthies" to save and protect. So when it turned out the Colemen were practicing Jehovah's Witnesses (the least forgiving of the winter-favored sects) residents of all stripes blew their gaskets, and the crudely charming pictograms—*woodprints*, the two Toms insisted, having the kit to prove it—were plumbed as symbols for all sorts of corkscrew plots and cultish in-ventions. Listening back, several in Frank's company agreed, it all sounded pretty silly. The kind of "rural hys-teria" their own mayor—Mayor Montenegro—had shut down for good. Enlightenment was everybody's own re-ward. They'd agree to agree on that, at least. To boot, Frank said, the press could never figure out which of the boys—Tom the Fair or Tom the Dark—had done the ac-tual drawings, and a mystery that trivial meant extra in-nings for *weeks*. "You know I could *feel* the waves of ten-sion and hostility—neighbor pitted against neighbor—like actual waves, washing up against my barber sta-tions—you know, the *chairs*." "Nobody could tell them apart?" asked Arthur Drake, one of the volunteer deputies. "Oh no, they weren't identical," said Frank. "In fact, I'm not even sure they were twins." Sandy had been known for her austerity and her stubbornness—a hard, sometimes beautiful woman. The story (which Frank was busy throwing water on) was that, when Sandy had twins—even though the two boys *looked* nothing alike —she figured she'd give them both the same name since she'd had the hardship of the pair of them, at more or less the same time, with the one name to demonstrate she would raise them alike in righteousness, there being but the one path to it.

Oh, the one path whereto *it*—*! Whereby two Toms side by side bring us to Otto's autumn. Too much? Oh no! For whatever reason, the brothers don't—or can't—get along, maybe it has to do with their sharing a name. Except for that and age, they have little in common, and each denies—or, for whatever reason, one takes on the role of older brother, the "younger" submits, and they try to pass, as best they can—given their mother's sense of justice, cruel, poetic or whatever: the redoubtable double ottotto—as normal brothers. Otto, the older*

*one, takes a protective attitude toward young Otto, basically
a coward who takes that protection as his due. Off they go! But
I babble—I babble because I am so goddamn afraid. There's
nothing else to live for here anymore.* If you can't live with
eyes in the back of your head, learn to live *without* them.
That's from the Collected Wisdoms of Fear, *Bearden
County Edition,* Tom's book of terrifying kinships—I can't
say more!—*he loves nothing better than to chew the barklike
pages like they were old-fashioned jerky. A bee sting is what I
think of when I see his last name, but infinitely worse—or
longer. Thimble. And I shared a first. As we shared, he will
always be reminding me. Otto (tomtom), the piper's son,
rough and tumble. He'd like me to think that, to believe there's
no hope, that he occludes it by being in perfect—immortal, he
would say—synchrony with me. Yes, but the immortality of
a dung beetle. One at a time. Symmetrical. Oh, how very symmetrical my oddly terrifying friend is!*

From an early age, the dark-haired Tom had despised his
fairer twin, whom he viewed as a complete phony, so
transparent and yet so successful in his manipulations
it laid plain to Tom, the dark one, the unbelievable gulli-

bility of people throughout B——, ordinary folks and eggheads alike, even his friends and his family, and because he would not—*could* not, on principle—disguise his hatred for this light-haired impostor, his "twin" brother, *he* became the one people mistrusted. *He* did, when, ironically, *he* was the boy and then young man of static yet piercing convictions. Maybe (just maybe) the thimble of a clue could have been extracted from Frank's tendentious account. Inspector Madison made notes to check on the official manifest of objects locked inside the 1974 BTC, but the revelations coming from the gazette—the double diary and its supernatural take on the hunting jacket (a shunting device from one nature to the next, or time)—put all that straight out of his head . . . until it was too late. Embittered, Tom's reflexes and sense of distances betrayed him at the ripe young age of twenty-nine, while driving on 47 south into Montrose, taking a corner too fast—loss of traction, socking his left lights into a tree—out his spirit poured, through the windshield of this world, and into the next. Following his brother's death, fair Tom changed—dissolution into somebody darker, less manly. . . . Some months later, he—always the successful, fair, seemingly well-adjusted one—left his job without notice, never calling in, not even to pick up his last check. He started to haunt the library. After a few months, it was clear his hygiene habits had gone downhill as well: whenever you saw him in public, he would be wearing the exact same jacket—getting more soiled and smellier by the day, and he would greet you pleasantly enough but with a tacit smirk, as though just by saying "hi" or "hey" or "how are you," he was being "normal." Happy houses. No—you could see in his eyes what had happened. A year and change after his brother's death, Tom gets into trouble with the law—clumsily waylaying a young girl, or attempting to. Taken before the judge (this time *without* his famous hunting jacket), he pleads bipolar, but old Dumfries doesn't buy it. Tom lands eight-to-twenty-five in county lockup. And here he was—a decade later, said Frank Reed. "That's justice for you." And that was some time before Mayor Monty and his Council of 24 figured out this "Tom" had been, in fact, *sent back* from the future, carrying the plague-in-two-parts: "contact/shock." The cards had been filched from the 1974 Time Capsule in order to clinch the illusion. Of course, by then it was too late. But, pause for a second . . . can you imagine that? Being born too late? Being told *Whoops, sorry kids! shit . . . uh, guess you were born* too late! Well, fuck—let's just *see* what these notes tell us … why *not* invent? For the sake of *their* precious posterity? We'll just see about that.

I woke suddenly—sapped out of blackness and suddenly —horribly—awake. I was standing at attention, staring blankly into my closet—nothing there but my clothes: a couple of dress shirts, some polo shirts, jackets, a few black and tan pants draped at the knees and a sheaf of ties taking up my wire hangers, as well as shoes, shoeboxes, and a plastic container with sliding lid holding socks in rolled-tight pairs. What was at the bottom of this? I wondered—what was I doing?—and, for that matter, what time of day—or what day, for that matter—was it?

After locating a reliable calendar, I understood my predicament and began to make calls.

My job was gone—they had replaced me the second time I failed to show. The good news was my modest reserves—a "rainy day" CD and a savings account—were untouched. I had enough to last me a couple of months—at least until I figured out the mystery of those missing days—days so perfect—and there seemed to have been dozens of them—they had passed in and out of consciousness without leaving any residue, a single memory. Nothing. I tried to locate clues that would jolt my memory and then—when I saw the blank wall I was facing—I gave up.

I kept to my bedroom, listened to the radio and read, pampering myself as if I were recovering from a serious illness, which I was, in a sense, a feeling reflected in the second paperback I started—an old-fashioned sci-fi job, The Genocides. There were so many typos I had to read the poor thing twice. Also, the "atmosphere" was laid on pretty thick for this sort of provender—could've used a little more animation. It was suggestive enough, however, to me, in my hypersensitized state. The plot concerned a county dealing with a mysterious plague. The efforts of county administrators—venal, small-minded, not terribly competent—to halt its spread, and when their efforts fail, the transition of the disease into an otherwise healthy populace, depictions of the ensuing panic. Within a relatively short period of time, the county dwindles down to a hundred or so survivors.

Physically, however, there was nothing the matter with me—nor was I psychologically affected as far as I could tell, aside from the—as one would assume—the almost malignant curiosity concerning that missing period. In my possession—or within easy grasp—were any number of clues—facts, suppositions, and so forth—to help me fill in at least a

few of the blanks, should I care to: the things "I" had done—
fed myself, left the house, used the car, being a few examples
satisfactorily figured out, then digested—and those things,
who knows why, in my somehow "anonymous" state—this
"'I'" was frightened, yes, perhaps—had not even attempted.
More than enough to figure out what had happened—but I
couldn't.

The answer had to be fed to me, in a sense—read.

Tom had slipped several note cards—one at a time, so that
*they were thoroughly interleaved—*oh, and that was so like
my brother!—*between the pages of the fifth book I happened*
*to pick up, a mystery of some sort—*Celestina, or The Wild
Seeds—*and several of them fluttered out, falling out of order,*
when I picked it up by the binding. Of course, I didn't see it all
at once.

Aha, I thought, notes (["I"]) must have written—well,
these ought to be helpful.

And then I thought—the handwriting isn't mine—yet fa-
miliar, weirdly enough.

And even then I didn't get it.

And then, when I did recognize the writing, I thought—
well, what's this *been doing here for so long?*

And then I looked at the fourteen small ruled cards ($5\frac{1}{2}"$
× $3\frac{1}{2}"$), which looked new.

And then I went back to the book, went to the flyleaf and

looked at the penciled "6—" where Sid had scratched in the price—ridiculous!—and I remembered when I had bought it—how I swore I'd never go back (aside from the ridiculous prices, he'd been bad-mouthing his customers again)—and how I had been looking forward to reading it right away, before—right where I lost track.

And I thought about this and went back to the closet, and I stood there, thinking and staring into it—thinking hard for a long, long time.

And then I checked the jacket pockets.

And later—no—how do you reconcile yourself to that borrowed issue?

The notes: " "

Card *1.* I never want to wake that suddenly again—snatched out of blackness and suddenly —horribly—returned to my senses. I was aware of my surroundings, and that they weren't familiar to me.

Card *2.* I am hard-pressed to say what happened next—later, of course, I would be able to calculate how much time had passed, just as I became expert in figuring out the gaps between my brother Tom putting on the—*my*—hunting jacket. That being my *first* concern, as you may imagine.

Card 3. Imagine being able to throw off the spell of living as easily as removing a jacket—with the possibility of returning to it as long as *he* for whatever reason decides to put it back on. Does he know—? By now—why, he *must!*

Card 4. Later I would imagine it as follows—a page folded in half, and that half folded again, compacted into a quarter of its original length, and so on, down to a piece that extended to almost nothing, but compressed to impossible thickness—a window the size of a dust speck, or a fleck of foam, a microbe of mortal consciousness, and this was me, this was the all I had become—the immanent state, a permanent nothing, or nothing but some horribly compressed, indivisible awareness—and I would imagine this speck a fleck at the foaming peak of an immense evolutionary wave. I forced myself to go for walks. Even when the temperature was in the 90s, I would walk around in "my" hunting jacket. As I walked, I would gaze at the specks of dust reeling in the sunlight—and, for just a second, I could imagine myself trapped inside one of them, staring out of its eyelet into this cruel, too-bright world.

Card 5. But there always came the day when I found I simply couldn't go on wearing the same jacket, day in and day out—and it wasn't the smell, though that was foul—and it wasn't the chafing, the rashes or the boils, or any of the other physical—I should say, *material*—discomforts, not even the personal contacts lost, with my few acquaintances and such, it wasn't anything material but an urge that grew even as I tried to stamp it down, grew and overtook me until I knew I had to risk everything—risk the void—or permanently lose my sense of reality or—*my rights as possessor.*

Card 6. I am afraid the blue sky will fall down on me—like poor Chicken Licken.

Are we there yet—? *"Go back to sleep," our father orders from the front seat. He looks over at my mother, who looks back at him with features inexpressible. Not love or yearning*—those I can express. Like so. Love. Yearning. *Note that Tom's little twin-within-a-twin tale makes no sense. The absurdity of individual facets, such as a mother like Sandy Coleman being allowed to keep her kids—it's almost insulting. Near midnight, but our father has dark shades on, even though he's driving—and so does mom, so the expressions they are giving each other, when he looks away from the road, briefly—she's constantly looking over at him, smoking like a chimney—a pretty, neurasthenic brunette with a hood-pouched ponytail—are especially hard to read from the back seat, in the dark—trying to get a better angle in the rearview mirror. That made sense, in any case—it's always 20/20 in hindsight.*

Because the left hand writes *I'm afraid the sky will fall down on me—can't seem to leave the house*—and the other hand writes *I'm always out—making up for lost time.* "To be made redundant by a hunting jacket," said the barber, on a collect call to his good friend Chuck, misunderstanding everything as usual. "My Jesus!" To spare himself an old embarrassment, Dr. Otis had gotten chummy with Frank Reed, much to his regret—more thorn than burr, the doctor amended, redundantly. In fact, what he'd read scared him half to death: *I've promised not to write about it (TT) anymore. If it's time for our twilight to begin, let it... begin the work of tomorrow—bidding us goodbye and burying us in time to hatch themselves in earnest! Hatching fast from our plots, our future creators—the children of these diseased, filthy, defective leftovers.* Dr. Otis thought he'd seen or heard it all. "So what?" people would say—the ones he dared to show it to. "It *looks* like nonsense—so he's nuts." But days later even unimaginative characters like Frank would be smitten with bad dreams or thoughts so unpleasant they couldn't sleep. Fears of supernatural agents and oversharers. The pathologist had to visit several booksellers in the Triple Cities area, but eventually he picked up a copy of the book Tom had written about, *The Genocides.* Not far in, he decided he could be reading about his own county of Bearden—with hardly any of the names altered. The *levels* of coincidence didn't even surprise him anymore. There was something about the troubles they were starting to see, warning signs of further subdivisions.

Later—the county in ruins: most of its citizens comatose and all but a few of the few remaining dead of the "plague"—seven months later, it would be understood by what remained of county authority—Mayor Monty among others, his newly installed deputy, Lane Phillips (he'd lost four since the crisis began) and Sir Charles Otis, now in charge of the surviving Parthenogenesis Team—that when former-deputy Smitty had flown in the specialists "from outside," he had also imported the more frightening of "the twins," as they came to be known.

The strange (if mostly harmless) sleeping sickness and the always fatal shock of paracounty contact.

Others felt this "contact/shock" from the Colemen's uncanny pages as well. "It's like concentrated evil, or bad luck—I started and then stopped right away." "Just *touching* them!" "Why? Because it made me realize that while I was out—*get it?* Out, so to speak—anybody could be doing anything! Who knows what kind of batshit crazy he's been up to?" Then, when the time came to pay (*play the pipers!*) he could simply *remove* the jacket and by the time one got oneself oriented, it would be too late, Tom could be hiding in the most ordinary articles of clothing, waiting to take one over. Shirts and blouses made the most sense—but then Tom wasn't exactly a *sensible* guy! You'd see people hesitate to slip on outerwear, especially—looking for mismatched items on others. Oh, what a cowardly but effective revenge! An entire county revised out of existence, or worse—*deliberately falsified* at a later point in time. Tom's doing us proud. Everything rendered wrong. He keeps making excuses—abstruse, aimless scenarios—because what he cannot face is that the brother who "possesses" him is indistinguishable—in personality and therefore *in fact*—from himself: neither Tom the darker, nor Tom the lighter, but Tom *the implausible.*

He was the scaredest little kid you'd want to meet. In addition to his own exhaustive-in-itself compendium, Reynold seemed

to be able to intuit and absorb *the fears and phobias of those closest to him—me, his older brother, his guardians and cousins, friends (he had a few) and family—making them his own. He was extremely thin, seeing as he had all kinds of food allergies.* "A nervous stomach," *our aunt would say—and others in her train—*"but a mighty eye." *Ever since I can remember—since Reynold was just a baby—people were remarking the quality of his eye. He was a baby—then an infant—for what seemed a long time. Six years? Maybe. In any case, when he was born, I was the elder by six years—but he didn't seem to stop crawling around on all fours until I was— oh, twelve? In his crib, he'd be teaching our grandmother his languageless lessons—squalls and whimpers that she could turn off by concerted patterns of action—gifts of fungible building blocks, mostly, and a reassuring number of pats, taps, belly farts, etc. We were left with her—our grandmother—first. My single memory of my parents seems to exist out of time.*

"You see," Otis explained, "many of the smaller wild mammals survived comfortably enough within their so-called civilized parameters—inside the human penumbra of consumption and waste, leftovers and dropped accidents—particularly the park creatures, the squirrels and pigeons fed by the old ladies and favored by our sunset connoisseurs—who grew to alarming numbers on the carelessness of human charity, and so were poised to *take over*, when things started to get tough for us." He was thinking about the paperback he'd just finished, which—whichever Tom's criticisms of it notwithstanding—had proved quite gripping. It helped pin down Otis's intuitions about the whole body-in-the-Woodwalker's-cabin affair. Namely, that far from doing a dissection the county should cremate the body *immediately*—and the notes. "Look out!" *The Genocides* seemed to be yelling at him, even though it offered no solutions. "Look ahead!" Maybe, Dr. Otis decided, just maybe, he could avoid some of his fictional counterparts' mistakes. They'd made so many, of course—and the book was iffy about which actions were mistakes and which appropriate-but-insufficient measures. Dr. Otis sent a priority memo to the mayor's council, offering his advice and underlining the important arguments many times, which probably didn't help his case. Life imitating, of course, it was stupidly ignored . . .

My sole memory of them seems to exist outside time—pulled from a dream I know it isn't. I'd swear to this. That is, if anybody cared. Belief's a funny thing. Out of nothing night would propose this darkness. But in an incomplete draft—nights felt unfinished, and therefore more human, in the country we knew as summer: *equivocal, half-asleep, aiming for the ghostly spheres behind the clutch of the stars—impossible ports of call. Reynold would be bunched up behind me, in the cargo-end of the olive-skinned family wagon, monopolizing the space with his Lego utopias. His breathing heavy—but he was a mouth-breather (and a heavy one at that) so it was hard to tell whether he was asleep or faking it like me. The eagerly timed sweep of sodium lights, mobbed with night insects. The headlights suddenly present behind us, the car's inside briefly backlit from shoulders up, passing alongside, then the bifocal embers disappearing ahead—elastic divinities, parallel and diverging, drawn entirely from light. Our car was one of them. We strained to hear our makers—our natural parents—above the race of driven air. Our mother seemed to rely for her support on father's convictions, habits, actions, interpreting what she could for our benefit.* Your father is whistling again. William, what are you whistling for? He's whistling because he's in a good mood. Kids, stop fighting! You don't want to ruin your father's good

mood, do you? *Or letting us know when they didn't matter:
You're muttering again. Can't you do that somewhere
else? The wind would string along bags and paper wrappers
from dinner—Carrols' club burgers with granular shakes
and vanilla-tasting fries—buffeting the cabin. They'd fed us
in the car—that had to be significant, I thought—because
we'd been driving for what seemed a long time. Headlights
splashed across billboard greens, big and small, too fast to
read. Eternity takes on funny shapes to a kid. I remember my
juvenile crystal-gazing and Bach's paracounty "Tweaker's
Trilogy," only . . . very vaguely—I don't know how to describe
these beliefs. The early false earth scenarios. The stars were
placeholders, merely, like our nervous systems were—
mother's, father's, Reynold's, my own—overlapping yet kept
inexplicably apart. Even on longer trips, we'd have to arrange
the suitcases so that Reynold could "set up" his traveling mu-
nicipalities in the back of the station wagon. Though he often
got his way, nobody would call my brother spoiled—the routines for placating him being so otherworldly. He suffered (a
mild form of) what psychiatrists were then calling Gerson's
Syndrome, which they sought control over with drugs that
pacified his anxieties and judgments, confrontation therapy,
and—when he turned teen—participation in the vanguard
Erhard seminars. The drugs were like "putting cotton wool"*

between his ears, he said, but they did calm him. He got into the therapy, felt it a mark of distinction for somebody his age, but the seminars he avoided any way he could—he thought they were cruel. I urged him to do as he was told. Secretly, however, I supported his rebellions, passive and short-lived though they were. I knew I suppose, or guessed, that he would-n't always be so opposed to the doctors' scientific treacheries in the guise of treatment. What did they know? Me? Him? We did what we always do. We hope for a way through. Better things to come . . . what seemed an eternity after night fell—midnight, or the small hours—we pulled off the highway lit at calming intervals, onto a cloverleaf ramp wrapped around a sloped lawn, in a sort of artificial bear hug, and onto the Parkway lit more makeshift—pop-up tungsten, the red-and-blue neon of the Skylark—the buildings smaller, or lower to the ground at least—a Swiss shack with a fruitseller's down-stairs and guitar shop above, a half-cylinder bunker of rippled tin now hosting movies—where, up the hill from the Present Company's all-white invite box, our parents would abandon us, and me and Reynold would enter The Story *(. . . my namesake's, of course).*

From *The Genocides:*

"The first time it flared up was in late July, very suddenly, fourteen dead in under a week, all of whom had been assigned—or otherwise connected—to the Coleman case. Panic, confusion—you better believe it! But before anybody had time to speculate too closely, the epidemic appeared to have burned itself out, and Montenegro had all the bodies cremated. Foolishly? Or to hide something incriminating?

"'We were obviously on the right track,' the mayor affirmed in his weekly press conference, 'we had to be—to have provoked this kind of response. And I'm not going to lie to you about the seriousness of this event—it's serious. I believe most of you out there know I lost someone close to me—a good friend and excellent colleague. Things look pretty grim now—pretty doggone scary—but, listen, we are coming at this from a position of strength, we really are, people—we have got some of the best minds in Sunnyside Hills working nonstop—around the clock. I promise—as I know all of you do, too—I promise not to quit—to double and redouble our county efforts, until I have discovered the source of this outrage, be it virus, bacteria, chemical, or human.' This last was by no means off-the-cuff. Aides leaked the mayor's conviction that these were poisonings—the work of a deranged or disgruntled scientist passed over for promotion or who hadn't been invited onto the Coleman research teams. Everybody knew how good Montenegro's instincts were when it came to human mischief.

"St. Smitty's successor, Scott Thomas was permitted a three-week 'honeymoon' by the local press of private and public interests, which was also (not coincidentally) our reprieve before the second outbreak—a much worse affair."

Storms and sirens stood tall in Reynold's pantheon of fears— or maybe they were it, *the source of everything. Sound that could blanket the entire county, swamping earth and sky like they were the same thing. Sound there was no getting rid of— escape from. It didn't matter that the sirens had a melody you could get lost in, or the storms were a bigger blast than all the fourths of July that year put together. Turning the countryside into this suddenly epic—epileptic—theater of misrule. How could you be a boy and* not *love a thunderstorm? Mindful of my father's last words to me—*Tom, *he said,* Tom, take care*

of your little brother—*I tried some "treatments" of my own for Reynold, with regard to his most crippling fears. I figured if I could isolate and magnify the germ of his phobic insanities at their root, I could do what I wanted with it—for example, scoop it out. Of course, I fucked up. Tom Tom, the piper's son. I planted a megaphone in our aunt's garden, and told him it was the* only *siren he need worry about anymore—that the sound issued straight from the Spirit of the Earth. By that I'd meant something Bach-tweaked, but Reynold misunderstood me—or understood at a level I, the possessor of the meaning, was as yet unaware of—with all too predictable results. I put a siren in the grass—and of course he* swore *he could hear sounds coming out. Scary voices. This garden was the least frightening place one could imagine—that I could, at any rate. Spiked yellow agrimony (the "best pillow-stuffer" in the county, our aunt claimed), protozoan clumps of white snow-drops, clover and geraniums, and trellised roses near the yard fence. The half-buried megaphone resembled a flower or the simplified symbol of a flower, with its lewdly thick pistil amid the weeds and wildflowers—Reynold would kneel on the wet grass in front of it, listening, watching—I dared not remove it. He was twelve so I must have been twenty-four by then. We were growing apart—I could feel it. He could feel it—he wriggled it out of me somehow, the whole mindful. It was bad* enough when I let Reynold take possession of my worst fears, but when I saw he was being influenced by other things as well—desires I kept hidden from the light, as best I could—I didn't know what to do. We'd been growing apart for years, it seemed. A beam of sunlight—drapes. I am prone to—well, get . . . —overexcited. Wipe the slate clean, I thought. So right when the hardware store opened, I was there, I bought several gallons of white latex, a brush, a roller, a tray—rummaged around for old newspaper. Same stinking plague. Same year it's been since we put the BTC to earth. Endless chains of summer. Our garden (but if only we'd known in advance!) of earthly delights. I didn't go to sleep until my wall was completely repainted—until all four coats had dried—and when I did, I dreamt of him—of the one I wasn't able to name yet and the tiny houses he moved into, between the pillow and sheets, he was inside all our houses, undermining our foundations, our wisdom, stealing our teeth, leaving worthless coins in their place, mistaking copious gobs of drool for rain—and when I woke, I discovered that the moths, lymantric despair, mistaking the white surface—blindingly white—for a starched shirt, had peppered hundreds of holes—like magnified braille—into my wall so recently repainted.

From *The Genocides*:

"This time thirty-six dead in six different locales—nine in Windsor, two in Slocomb, seven in Kiamesha, four in Caberville, three in Placid Prospect, three in Upgrade, five in Bundt Valley—and among six very different hill and valley sets. Again it took everybody it struck with a speed and finality as though those afflicted had been selected in advance. It was, opined Otis, neither an air-, insect- or water-borne pathogen. The havoc it wreaked played leapfrog. It skipped about like a malicious child—like something having fun. A furious spurt of activity, then rest . . . This time, a relatively short one: it was early September, just after Monetenegro had closed the border (a toothless decree, for there were no reserves to enforce it) when the 'plague' returned, and the bills for this third and worst-by-far outbreak showed '739 infected—0 spared.' For it was terminal in every instance, once the symptoms became evident—a matter of thirty-six hours, typically. And always—like a drumroll, if you will—in the same sequence, aches, chills, fever, erratic pulse, hair loss, rashes, nausea, vomiting, diarrhea, lymphatic swelling, supplementary abscesses, hallucinations, the skin peeling off and then liquefaction of nervous members leading to severe internal bleeding—

blood loss through each orifice—always fatal and with very drawn-out penultimatums."

Afraid of spiders. Squadrons of ants. Mosquito bites—his fears began once he was bitten. Afraid of snakes, even those not seen in-county. Concomitant fear of shrubbery, tall grass, undergrowth. Afraid of the woods—especially the woods past our back fence, thin as it was, mostly birch. Afraid of the spiderlike vibe of willows, weeping especially. Afraid of rain or hail—when the sky was a particular arm's-length from gray, any precipitation would do. Afraid of the dark. Scared of curds. Afraid of dark cumulus. The backs of refrigerators. That was one of mine—I'd had a nasty surprise in my grandmother's basement when I was—oh, I don't know. Afraid of falling wreckage from midair plane collisions. Dark water—ponds, lakes and pools you couldn't see to the bottom of. Afraid of small holes and large pores. Too afraid to stand under telephone wires. Scared of slipping on small stones on the way to the water tower. Afraid of broken bones—compound fractures in particular. Afraid of the tower. Afraid of fossils, of shells ebbing into rock—the aeons relative to human history. Fear of aeons. Fear of distant relatives. Afraid of quarantine.

Of the eternal prosaic. Afraid of fear itself. Metaphobia. Claustrophobia. Agoraphobia. Hydrophobia. Geminiphobia. Philophobia. Acrophobia. Poganophobia. Xenophobia. Algophobia. Heresyphobia. Astrophobia. Brontephobia. Thassalophobia. *Afraid of disease and of day-to-day sicknesses, for fear they could turn into real wasting diseases. Afraid of fire. Afraid of eraser rubbings. Black cats. Volcanos. Afraid of locked doors—of being forced to open one in particular. Afraid of July 4. Afraid of bulldogs with ragged smiles stretching back to their ears. Fear of beards. Afraid of strangers. Afraid of the branches of trees, especially when spoken to. Afraid of borders and outlines drawn by misshapen hands (another fear he got from me). Fear of cheap paper-packs—pages falling out terrified him especially. Afraid of squashes, carved pumpkins—everything to do with Halloween. He was afraid of most holidays except Christmas and his birthday. Movies with R ratings—just the poster for* Power of One *gave him nightmares for weeks. Frightened that everything is false, wrong, won't work out. Fear of failure. Fear of ether. Fear of garbage—the filthy cans. Frightened of dogs who were too friendly. Afraid of hamsters, but not gerbils or white mice. Fear of going blind—deafness not so much. Afraid of certain kinds of textures, like fruit churned up from the bottom of the yogurt cup. Afraid of Jell-o. Afraid of stuffed animals. Afraid of assassination. Barking dogs. Wilted lettuce. Afraid of extremes. Fear of symmetry.*

A chrysalis-like unfolding. He'd been sent back to become the first *Change Agent*, and from the success and *example* he made of Bearden, many more "subdivided counties" were to follow. An example of things going right—*horribly* right—for a change. From certain angles he was almost handsome—at others, his face seemed too small for his features. *He went off to spread the word that the world was lost—from here on, only counties.* Half-pint . . . Shortstuff . . . Goober. Tom Thimble.

What nobody could cure—not with drugs or therapy—was the overempathizing routines he'd succumb to, the absorptions and their necessary emetics. Empathy is a paradoxical word, because Reynold had a hard time recognizing the foundation stone of other people's existence—pain, suffering, etc.

His routines were stiflingly selective. But he was dedicated to—no, driven to create, just as I am—those early forms: key influences on Reynold's "mature" architecture. A master-builder with a fascinating eye, as everyone claimed—from the start, he had a talent for placing things into piles whose beauty and logic would require ten minutes of careful concentration before becoming plain. It was no surprise he wanted to be a city planner when he grew up. Building his own perfect world, block by block—perfect for the conveyance of all his pet phobias, and us, I fear—us he more or less anthropomorphized, but reluctantly so that even his pets took notice. No—no! But what was surprising was how little he took to Escher when I bought him the book for his ninth birthday. It hurt my feelings—made me wonder.

It's difficult now to convey how desperate those times were—and how strangely B— (or "Sunnyside Hills," the change M. Montenegro made in his first one hundred days in office, capturing history—the B-dash thing was just "too *gloomy*," he said) was altered. The attempts by first the wealthy and then the general populace to flee the area—the tributary actions of an outside reserve force, for bad and for worse—the various routes to disaster amid the pretense to righteousness by some—the ascendancy of charlatans, fortune-tellers, false prophets, astrologists—the miraculous cures touted by a new generation of quacks and complaint-disposers: the acupuncturists, phlebotomists, holists, chiropractitioners—the many routes narrowing to one, a judgment in flames and writ large—the pursuit of frivolous or bestial arts: the paint-huffers, pill-seekers, pipetail-suckers, exhibiters of filth—the dodges and expediencies of the merchant classes—the daily rumors (the more farfetched the better) debunked and yet irrationally maintained—the occasional news from outside.

Lapses in logic . . . lapses in sense.

His kindnesses follow a peculiarly subterranean order—how small they are compared to the cruelties they so fleetingly suppress. Kindnesses? He is my chief torturer, who laughs at and lords over me our present incapacities. I raise a hand to stop him—but it's the wrong one—and nothing helps, because whichever way I go, he's written it off first, from a distance impossibly remote . . . my brother in time . . . he hatches,

will hatch, from my remnants decades on, a beetle the size of a—no, I won't say it! It isn't true! *We are both young—indeed my creator's future is still unborn!—and yet we haggle over the threads and sinews of our different accounts—our loathsome transaction—with the sentimental hunger of old men, as if the only book worth a damn in our dismal "do-over" of a universe, the only one worth swapping, is the book made out of human skin.*

TOO LATE

GUIDING LIGHTS

To die is more than difficult dreaming, papa would drill into her, *or difficult words,* Margaret listening without participating, not wanting to understand more than she did already. The topic unsettled her, and her mind would wander ... ever since she could remember, she'd been listening to her mom's outraged stories of the sister born a few minutes after her. How much time was enough to do serious damage? Ida, Margaret's little sister by minutes, arrived into this world by nature defective—incapable of tracking motion, handling objects, or learning county English. Lilian had blamed him, most of all. Her husband. For ruining her luck. For not saving their daughter. When the time came, he'd been too afraid to openly challenge Bearden's Registry, although he claimed different of course. "Coward! Quisling! Collaborator!!" She had the odd word at her beck. The brain damage was obvious to both parents by the close of Ida's first year, and their success in concealing it until Ida was three guaranteed both a scandal ("plain as day to *me*, and *I'm* no census-taker!") and a movement to strengthen and reform county registration procedures: new trainings/allocations. Registry turned the Maxwell case over to Magistry, who—in consultation with the independent umpires—made the difficult call. Sterilization for Lilian, for placing personal needs above the county's. And next winter, Ida would have to "find her own shelter." What that meant for a defective girl of three, of course—oh, "the rules of three"! They'd recovered her easily enough, at the start of spring, moments from where she had been left, caterwauling: on the southern flank of Ingraham Hill, halfway inside a warren where a fox or canine had dragged her. Lying on the couch with a compress against her forehead, suffering fatigue and migraine, Lilian Maxwell would retail all of it to Margaret, who was too young to fully comprehend, sparing nothing. Of course, neither she nor her husband, Henry, had seen the body. Although she believed it would have been better not to have to imagine. She described how the imaginings haunted her dreams, disturbed or interrupted her hibernation. A confused, vindictive, powerfully unhappy woman: the more Margaret could remember, the more she suspected her mother blamed the loss on her, Margaret, as well. In physical appearance, she took after her autodidactic papa and didn't resemble her little sister, intellectually or physically, in any way. Physically, Ida had resembled their mother, Lilian … a harassed, perpetually frowning beauty, dissatisfied, thwarted, waiting for life to vindicate her. How? She didn't know.

Before the garden, she had remembered very little of her childhood—despite the rituals papa had imposed upon her, three times a day: oblations, invocations, burnt offerings… the gradual smoothing away of routine, and the disquiets indifferent to routine: moods of a certain thickness or swing, the glow of her ring, colors like ripe mooncloth … olive topaz … eggwhite mist, etc, etc. When she was young enough to be naïve, Margaret would imagine matching mood-glow to ring … while other people might own watches, she had her very own temper-keeper—*kemper* for short.

Blamed her, but at the same time Lilian Maxwell worried constantly about her surviving child: Margaret was the source of all her worries, just as her husband served for bitterness, and she drove herself to distraction, with one or the other, circling, harping. Up until the stroke that killed her—just higher than the county median, at age forty-seven—Lilian Maxwell had worked as a compressor of meats in Chester Carroll's factory below Ridley. She crewed Wednesday to Saturday, as part of a "coveting gang" he'd picked up from the county for cheap. On the days she worked, she would often bring home the damaged pressings, overseasoned tubes of flesh— pig, trout, chicken, cow—for their evening's cold buffets. "Your mother is a fine cook," Henry Maxwell would say to his daughter, before the pre-meal recital. "You should try to persuade her to make you her famous cabbage succotash." "Must you take me to task for *everything*!?" mom replied to papa directly, ignoring Margaret. Later, while washing up or toweling the dishes dry, Lilian would communicate to Margaret privately: "Your father wants you to think *he* is the victim in all this." Never—hardly ever—in front of Henry. Margaret had grown up with this dynamic of misdirection locked in place, for as long as she could remember . . . a snobbish, spoiled, bewildering child entering her mature estate, she had studied the pair of them—mastered their true and false notes—and then forgotten. Why? Because that's the way it is in Bearden county ... until one day it isn't the same red-and-white check tablecloth anymore. Her mother had six identical ones, three patched and stained, three for special occasions. A solitary drop of blood on the white "shag" carpeting of Margaret's bedroom, where her mom had gone to lie down—something she had started making a habit of, after work, returning to fight with her husband or daughter, paralyzed by rage or panic, depending. Dinner meats served with heads of Bibb, sliced cucumbers, carrots, and alfalfa, from papa's garden. Henry Maxwell possessed a *green thumb* ... another thing passed from father to daughter. There would be fresh wildflowers in the vase. "Observe that all individuals must recur at least twice," he would read—the same passage from his favorite tome, *What's to Be Done?!*, which Margaret knew by heart, not through any engagement or application of her own, but because of the inescapable recitations. Without clearing up, Lilian Maxwell excused herself and went upstairs to Margaret's bedroom ...

She had looked so tired—*beaten down*—when she walked away from them that last time. Margaret's dad tried rousing her a half-hour later. Why didn't he just let her sleep? Had he sensed something was wrong? He would deny premonitions of any kind. It was a complete surprise to him—as it was to Margaret—whereas her mother had vocalized her forebodings often enough. "What will you do when I'm gone?" she had inquired of them. "How will either of you survive?" Neither her husband, Henry, nor her daughter, Margaret, had any idea she'd meant this *literally* . . .

Papa was just as peculiar, in his way. In fact, a case could be made for his being worse, something the loss of her mom helped Margaret discover, or gain insight into—it was something she'd *always* felt, without putting into words. Polite, pedantic, a sedentary reserve rooted not in any specific feature—the mouth-purse or crow's-feet, the small head with its slovenly tonsure, the eyes partly veiled behind sun-correcting lenses—but in papa's presence as a whole, even *at a glance* . . . a summary impression his taut and watchful influence belied. Ever since Margaret could remember, he'd been involved in the printing and distribution of seditionist *tracts*, recycling Marks, Angel, Darkman, and Floyd. In theory, a crime deserving banishment, as in theory any crime was. By custom, Magistry was given the widest latitudes. How often would he recite his tracts before lunch and dinner? It seemed he was still courting his wife, in a way—working her appetite for irritation. The pair of them unappeasable . . .

For a while, their "guiding light" had been the Hopping Madman, who peddled a contemptible *false earth*-type philosophy tweaked just enough to avoid being shut down, during his twice-weekly conversation group, Landmarks in Chatter. The entrance was off a magnolia-shaded alley parallel to Endicott's Main Street, facing a sun-brightened parking lot. In those days, there were three telephone poles per block. Rows of collapsing metal chairs of a base talc color, twelve or so deep, covering the width of the auditorium. The central aisle. The combed and oiled hair-parts of the men like her papa, like all county supers had. She remembered the cloth-draped podium, where they sat off to the side, to observe the Madman's rant and dance routines. A dark-yellow curtain behind them with the county seal, a glittering carbuncle that pinned the two halves. The crackling shorts of the microphone, shunting his voice between blast and whisper. To a child of nine, the words bore no meaning, and once Margaret had worked out where the worst shocks were, she turned her attention to her parents—papa's panics, mom's sour amusement and hatred throughout. It had been Henry's idea. As always, his hopes betrayed him. After the initial visit and Henry's nervous indigestion, Lilian had insisted on their becoming regulars . . . "as a *family.*" Something about the Madman's bellicose antics appealed to her, and her husband's poorly disguised dismay made it all the more satisfying. A boredom so inbred it had made Margaret afraid, finally. She remembered bouts of yelling. Singling out members of the charter for tribute or abuse, at the Madman's leisure, but always *giving them voice.* He was "hopping mad" about one thing or another . . . that went with the name. He demonstrated his outrage with a dance that suggested a hotfoot, deftly shifting from foot to foot as he remonstrated, roared, and explained, all the while soft-stepping diagonally across the stage with his microphone and his lassolike cord. "I'm hopping mad about such and so ... !" he would yell of a Thursday. Sundays were the more raucous affairs. "I'm hopping mad about these October pranksters!" Or these "August eggheads!" He would yell about his theories and displeasures, and the audience would come alive. These were frightening moments for an inward-looking child like Margaret (who could also sense her papa's tenseness ...), but she quickly learned to predict them, and mark out their proscribed limits. When she was older, she found some satisfaction in learning about the Madman's finish ... —how he had overstepped in one of his hatreds connected with the Allen regime, and disappeared from his berth during the final winter of 2006, only to be discovered later, drawn and quartered, a torso and the five appendages dispersed throughout the county—within the larders and canning cellars of a select and extremely scared bunch of citizens.

While Margaret's mom related her grievous life history, her papa read to her from seditious books. He told her about a little prince who lived on his own planet—a planet the size of a grapefruit. He read to her about a girl who followed a rabbit down a hole. She didn't like that one much. She learned the names of flowers, weeds, trees, grasses from him ... learned which plants were the natives and their wanderings to and fro, and which "exotics" were available "for a price" from the county nurseries.

She'd discovered the peeking hole at the age of six. *Once there was only "the garden,"* he made her repeat, *now there is so much more.* Chancing upon it in the narrow crawl space off the first-floor spandrel, following her first miraculous discovery of the world between the walls of their house. A carefully bored hole, at just the right height. The scenes she had witnessed before she was of age to understand, her own body following suit. Papa attacking mom ... restraining her with his barrel chest. Margaret's mother submitted with her usual show of bitter impotence, angrily raising an outstretched arm every so often. That's how Margaret interpreted it, at the time. Now she viewed this gesture in a much stronger light . . . yet not guiding, no, it was far too ambiguous for that. The painting in her parents' room, which would hang over this spyhole many hours of the day, had its provenance in East Branch, apparently: a hamlet in a county several counties east of Union. Unprovable, of course: for all of Margaret's papa's "evidence," it was still just a name (and sighting) on a speculative map. The scene depicted the eerie calm before a storm—although the storm seemed to be there, almost, already . . . it was hard to know. The lightning streaks in the top middle-left looked like wind-bent branches of trees, dancing but upside down. Two children were offering something to a small pony with a white star on its forehead, who was stretching its neck toward—perhaps sniffing—an unseen object. An adult riding bareback watches from his perch. The human figures are shapes filled by mixed shades of color, no two the same. Her father called it *The Gift*, but Margaret felt certain he'd made this name up himself. She knew the painting by heart because she studied it every time she attended to her parents' shrine, three times a day, in the northeast wedge of her hothouse garden . . . as proscribed in the seditious *tracts*

papa devoted his life to. A conservative spray of lilac
rood on either side of the scrolls, and scents. Since starting there, Margaret had always thought of it as "her garden," although the greenhouse belonged to the county.
She shared it with four other BOCES botanists, two ag-
researchers and a tiny female administrator named Lisa
Hurlbutt, whose last name was a torment to her. Now it
really did belong to Margaret, for the duration of the
winter. Black haw or stagbush, coming into fruit in the
artificial summer, produced the large, sweet blackber-
ries she filled two jelly jars with, and a bottle of astrin-
gent wine or vinegar— ... she didn't taste it to decide.
The interior was parceled into ten lots, eight roughly the
same size and shape with two smaller ones off the center. She spent November and December digging up—rotating—her plant beds, prey to an indecisiveness she
blamed on her nervous stamina. Perhaps it was a way to
justify how much time she spent there. The air inside
smelled fortified and strangely ageless. Flowering
cresses, ferns, miniature succulents hung censerlike
from the struts of the dome. Butter lettuces frilled the
eastern lots. Next to them (running clockwise) were purple radishes, bile-salt cucumbers. The only thing she

didn't rearrange (besides what ritual demanded) was the shrine guarding Henry and Lilian Maxwell during their respite in the *second nature*, which she'd moved in at the start of her service. Without interrogation, the customs officer had granted the necessary permit ... she'd remarked on the ease of the transaction—a remarkable thing—and he shrugged, and stamped her *veteran allowances* pamphlet. He wasn't being asked for an opinion. The painting was her only "personal" accessory for the shrine, and the more she thought about it, the harder it was to see the spirit in which she was offering it up, whether for meditation or sacrifice. It presided over the smoke of the incense, the gilt-framed photographs of her parents, the heavy clipping-and-samples album open on the homemade altar, over Margaret's moodswings ... a seasonal wreath of holly.

Observe that all individuals recur—occur, as it were, at least twice. The tradition of courting the dead places an incubus into the mind of the living. Study of such necromancy reveals an immediate and obvious distinction: that the raising of the

dead serves to glorify the struggle anew; that it fosters within
the imagination an aggrievement of the set task, not flight
from its solution, a rediscovery of the spirit of true evolution,
rather than a summoning of its ghost.

According to Marks (according to Margaret's papa), this "second nature" is limited by the mortification period, the decay of memory competing with the physical aspects. Resource conservation, which is much tighter within the second nature, won't permit passage of a full person, only those qualities consigned to the survivors' memories, such as they are. Thus enlightened by Marks, Maxwell had figured out a way to *select* these postmortem remembrances, asserting control over his continuance in the afterlife. He'd chosen his daughter, Margaret, to be the repository for himself and his wife, Lilian, after she'd left them. He became obsessed by this task ... everything he could squeeze in, memories he'd spent half of Margaret's life introducing, impressing ... engineering. From disbelief to—"Wait a minute," said Margaret, interrupting a lesson. "What's wrong?" he asked. "I don't think I can look at you the same way again." Papa lost his temper: "How dare you speak to me like that! What is *wrong* with you—!?" But the thing Henry Maxwell resembled most—when not attending to the shrine or to Margaret's training—was some form of shrubbery. Yew. Grim hours sitting in a chair. While hypocritically banning *her*, he smoked all the time, at the kitchen table, using a saucer for an ashtray, without leaving more than six butts which he could fashion into new cigarettes—an easy-pick blend of dandelion, hops, clover and mint. He wasn't chain-smoking. Usually he broke each cigarette down into segments of three, and he could wait up to an hour for the next smoke, but that was all he was doing . . . waiting. Whenever Margaret arrived in the kitchen where he sat, then he would keep smoking—lighting one off the other, impassively perfecting his technique. The smell reached everywhere, even into the closets. All of them (except the bedroom) filled from floor to ceiling with boxes, cans and jars and fancy clothes, everything her mom had won, cheated for or stolen and stockpiled from the Present Company over the last—. . . in fact, neither of them knew how long Lilian's hoarding dementia had gone on for. Perhaps he was too busy tormenting Margaret to wonder. Adding new "essentials." Sadly chastising her for the memories she'd already forgotten, or remembered so vaguely it would hardly count. Explaining the consequences of Margaret's inattention for both himself and her mom during their sojourn in or as second nature. Explaining to Margaret her duty. Wearing her down through their mutual sense of guilt and his unappeasable loss. Walking her through the house to identify trigger-objects, whereby erecting a duplicate "house" in her memory. Consciously imitating her mom, Margaret would cram everything into the closets of this "house" as well. Maybe it started unconsciously. The receipts Lilian wrote out by hand and hung upon every object—the estimate of worth. She'd saved every part of "the packaging," in pristine condition. Boxes and bags neatly folded, with the issuance of colored paper pressed into place inside. The figurines were the worst—the gnomes and trolls and processed dwarfs. The pain is so sudden and sharp it's frightening, but passes through his spleen quick enough. Even when the blood tars his stools, and in spite of near-constant pain, he looks forward to his coming departure from present company. Only now he worries about his daughter's loyalties ... *has he secured her submission?* Will she remember anything at all? Enough? "I will be pretending I am no longer here. And you—what are you going to do?" He repeats himself, anxious for his daughter's reply. She notices a moth alight on his left wrist, its will hypnotized by his cooling quiescence. The wings swing open and shut against its thoracic hinge, with a mindless shudder. "I will pretend you are," Margaret replies, but papa doesn't seem to be satisfied . . .

Henry had given her the power to destroy him and his wife, Lilian, her mom, once and for all, the lonely *power of one*, and now that she's understood how *wrong* he was about everything—just about everything to do with their county and the next, and all the possibilities of others, neighbors or no—Margaret realizes she no longer has any lights by which to guide herself and nothing to lean on, no principles of support. The price of induction. It's as if the countryside has fallen under her spell . . . or is "illness" more proper? She stared and stared and all the signs stared back, admitting nothing. A herd of cows, necks angled to the stingy grass at their feet. A maple tree growing inside a silo, branches twisting out through the slats. The days took their toll, awake to confirm it, to set the tone for her lack of preparedness, familiar tasks and tremors, to save and protect as much as possible, to try to remember, to ensure her parents' successful entry into the third nature together, hand in happy hand. A first snowfall that presently sank out of sight, but the second fanned across a night, a day and a night, shaking three feet of powder out easy, over the whole county. And they would stay that way—blanketed in its cold innocence, wires down, without electricity—until the following spring . . .

BETWEEN MOONS

1. THESIS

By peril, I don't mean what most people mean by the word. On the other hand, when I say I live in the future, this is pretty close to what most people mean when they say I, we, live in the present, in other words, existing in the moment or for the now, except with me that *now* is always *to be*, always precipitant or –tating, I'm not sure which: something purposefully aflutter, in any case, even in a state of repose. But I don't want to get ahead of myself, only to explain why this entry log won't carry dates, stardates, what-have-you. Dates have become an obsolescence in the future. I could fake them, of course, and have, for my colleagues or patients, for the sake of their mental complacency. My "fellow-travelers": now there's a term to wonder about. Right off the bat, I realized I could make up any date I pleased, and nobody would notice a discrepancy, even if I was asked twice or several times in a session. The nature of our confinement short-circuits memory without help on my part, although I did help, I helped my fellow-travelers along, to forget a little bit more each day, for a little bit longer, whenever I could, at first, while they were still living the same nightmare future-present as myself, as a kindness to them, to us all. As for me, I did myself no favors, I took the opposite tack: *nootropism.* I grew into my memories as a plant grows toward the light, remembering those crossed-out, reworded, rubbed-away phantoms of real feeling. By *right off the bat* I mean less than a century, that I'm sure of, which is why I use it instead of *over time* or *after a while,* phrases which could make a grown man weep. By *pretty fast,* I mean anywhere from ten minutes to ten years. I am able to say where we are, however, according to the ship. Stranded between Altairtwo I and Altairone II, the twin moons orbiting the planet Nodabendabon IV in the system named after the mortal half-brother, Castor. Here he sleeps, wakes, sits up, rubs his eyes: six stars in aphasic alignment, if the navigators' star-charts are accurate, and I very much doubt they are. There are so many things wrong with that last sentence I don't know where to begin. But don't imagine these are names I've made up myself, I'm not in the habit of assigning names to astral bodies, however new or well-intentioned they may be. And by orbit, by the way, I don't mean some pebble whipping stupidly round on a string but closer to a *Möbius* trip, by which I mean both one-dimensional and touch-and-go, placing the ship and its travelers in tremendous existential peril.

It happens pretty fast: one month later, he's back. I'm seeing Muncie repeat on the monitors. Later? Minutes? I would guess yes.

Because the "ship" carries no ports or windows to gaze in wonder out of, I can't describe the eagle, crab, rosette nebulae we've no doubt drifted past, nor our present eccentric orbit, in the Aabbab subdivision of Castor, fluctuating with the white blues of an ice ring or asteroid belt, no doubt some contorted labor of love between the two, not even the birth of the suprachiasmatic nuclei (SCN) which proliferate in the solar rainbow unbending around us, like dandelion spores. Cameras and recording devices bound to the hull, just as they honeycomb the hubs, corridors, air- and person-shafts within, a tremendous compound eye, or *composite*, something I don't like to think too much about, directed to my personal attention or perception, if I so choose. Inside, I no longer have a choice. Monitoring my fellow travelers and their I-won't-call-them "activities," they're nothing like my own, while tracking the endless stacks of hallways in this floating genius I choose to call *ship*, and which from the outside resembles nothing so much as the vicinity formerly known as The Heart of B— and its Grand River Plaza. I'd worked there, once upon a time. As the psychoanalytic head of a whole department of *psych-evaluators*, I was responsible for the mental health (and hygiene) of a small army of employees. Our offices in what had been the public library, a big book of a building stripped of its pages inside long ago.

Some time after we crossed into Castor everything *meta* started turning up Bearden County. Muncie on the heterodimensional monitor BMAL-1 was the first sign, a transcription activation I initially mistook for observer error, hallucination, what-have-you. The other way to go didn't check out either: somebody *like* Muncie moving around. Moving at a normal clip, for one thing, wearing the uniform of the past, for another, and third, somebody who didn't resemble a crew member: if I believed any of these three things, why not believe in all three and the inferential synthesis that made Muncie as well?

What the hey. All or nothing. I'm reasonably sure it was the BMAL monitor the first time. I took great care in noting where, and on which monitors, hetero- or homodime, Muncie (and then you) would appear, but it's hard when I can't keep my own records. Our devices have no communication or storage modes, although they do possess their own memories, nothing like our own, of course. I am as responsible as anybody for this ... after our communication devices abandoned us during our time of greatest need, without a second thought, who could blame us for not wanting them on board? Of course some would argue that the ship itself was one such device writ big, I'm sure I don't know. Everything here works by analog, by which I mean analogy. Early on I was told the science was beyond my grasp, and when I examined their "papers" or listened to the proud "parents," engineers and designers, talk among themselves, I realized they were right, it was utterly beyond my ken, although I also realized, quickly enough, that they had put this system (whatever it was) beyond theirs as well. In brief, we'd made ourselves obsolete: unable to "interface" with the devices which plagued the ship, by combo-monitors, speakers, or even the vaporizers triggering nanodorous memories. We couldn't communicate with each other or the ship, check its status, not even simple matters like self-flush, at least not without disconnecting these devices from the nucleus, and why would anybody do that? We'd be dead within a week without them. In other words, I'm not able to *see* what I tap on even as I'm typing it, although the ship possesses a sophisticated *autocorrect* function, so I've been told, so good it's said it has the ability to protect us from ourselves, or each other, although I have good reason to doubt this particular truth, as I will explain but not in this entry or theoretical future, even though I have a "keyboard" and a "screen" and I tap and I tap on it and nothing appears on it, it's very strange.

I wish I wish I wish I wish I wish I wish upon a star . . . instead, Muncie.

Heterodimensional BMAL-1 I can recall because I was checking it for radiation-readouts of Nodabend-4, which were through the roof. Unstable and with six suns beating down . . . what did we expect? Was this always our destination? A course setting I wasn't privy to? The planet with the light that burns. Breathe out, you're liable to combust. I don't want to think what happens when you breathe in. Even though I devised a way to set down notes about which monitors Muncie had last appeared on so as to identify a pattern, using an ingenious set of "writing" "implements" and "surfaces," my transcriptions vanished whenever I left them alone. (Our suits didn't have pockets.) There was a lot of vanishing going around, I noticed, including my decelerated fellow-travelers. Gone on the homodimes. Gone when I went to the compartment to visit in the flesh. Only to return the next time I checked. I queried the ship. Again, I felt like I was being asked or ordered to recall, no, *relive* an experience I don't need to work hard to ... "again," did I tap all this out before?

Many returns later, you join Muncie on the ship's screens as well. After a while, I remember your name. Genevieve ... for pity's sake. So I'm writing you (if you will) in this time of utmost peril ...

Tap tap, does tap, the tattle-tale heart: "I'm going to show you the seamy side of space," I tapped in or out, then waited years for your reply, if by years, if by reply, if by you, etc.

* * *

Genevieve. Sometimes it's you. Phased so near my own space-time continuum, STC, maybe a bit faster like Muncie is, fast, slow, it doesn't make a difference, really. Doing my best to hypnotize you in heterohomocombo, to bring you into my domain, so to speak, but we both know I have no power there. The opposite, if anything: the more I try, the more I seem to belong on your channel. Being near you makes me so dizzy. So . . . so . . . I remember. I remember because it's important. This is important. Going to lie down after another 101-hour shift, I nearly come into contact with this decrepit, maladroit, crazy-eyed old dame. She claims she's been here before, when she was hardly older than a girl. A teenager? I believe I'm beginning to understand. I needed a uniquely special being. A Lewy body to have and hold. A port in the storm. From dead air, I drew you here: *nootropism*, certainly. But why *your* memory? We had no special thing, I wasn't particularly attracted to you, and I couldn't believe you'd thought about me. We just happen to share the same past, you, me, Muncie and Philip, all eleven of us: our group encounter with the "ghosts of Bearden" while riding the purest acid manufactured on the eastern seaboard of our different states of the time, although back then I believe they were united, Knicker-bocker Glory. So ... when you disappeared with the other two girls, you got sent here. But Muncie was found the next day, crazy and incoherent, like the rest of us, but in the flesh. (Try as I might, I can't remember what "his story" was.) So ... this log's meant for *you*, you know, to stabilize the things I enter, for you to read back the strange truths I can't myself, only tap out, play forward, improvising these scary parlor games, turning myself into a repetopath or -tap, something merely language or mere machine ... a primitive tapping device.

And, oh, my heart, oh my heart, my heart—! You did reply, a year and a millennium too late ... now that it's time to reset the others: settle scores and impostures. Is that it? Is the future truly out of my hands? Because *that's* the question I'm asking. In a different entry, by playfully folding the back cover, I'll return myself to our vanished hopes for the past, and when I do I'll tell you all (all of you) where I'm from. But will you believe me? Accept me? Get scared and run? Take pity? What? Because that's the question I'm asking.

II. ANTITHESIS

Starlog no. 1.000001. By way of resource conservation, I took actions that would horrify some while earning the lasting praise of others, once the future I presently inhabit fails. Some others: my future creators, in a sense, in the sense of *how will they judge me* when they return to this STC? As a monster? Or their savior? The ship was LEED-sustainable, built-in even before we knew how the city blocks would transform themselves, but LEED could only take us so far. I saw another way to save on oxygen, sustenance, recycling, savings obligations ... enough to stretch survival to putative infinity? I decided to risk it. By then everybody acknowledged the cryogenic option hadn't worked out. It took longer than it should have because egos were involved, important egos, which I took a hand in deconstructing, I had no choice, beginning with our cocommanders and their marriage of happy convenience. Terry and Roos, bossy and playful, ponytailed votive worshipers, tossing the ball of command genially back and forth. I was sparing them (the whole crew) the recidivisms of an institutionalized old age, I rationalized. From my future vantage, I also admit sparing myself their realization that I hadn't been aging at the same rate. Would they have believed my answer? Had the least inkling of how *nootropism* operates? By rigorous meditation and growth toward the stable light of home, I'd gained some control over my basic metabolic functions, and was able to entrain both circadian *and* infradian clocks far beyond their normal rhythms. It was an inner-directed thing, and without the *meta*-earths, my fellow-travelers would have kept aging at the same pace over the course of our voyage as they had on earth, while I looked and stayed their junior by twenty years to the day. In short, they wouldn't have believed a word. In their shoes, would I? So I had no choice, by which I mean, of course, once I'd chosen my specific plan of action concerning *resource conservation.* I had no choice will always mean that. Once I'd decided to risk it, my routines became dopp-simple even as I was being run ragged. Four hundred and sixty-seven is a lot for one man to administer. I even considered "requesting" a couple of doppelgangers, but quickly thought better of it. First, there was no telling how the ship would recognize this request. Would it "take sides"? (But what did that mean? I was literally harming nobody. I don't think the ship, insofar as I construe a single entity as such, approved my particular course of action, but it didn't argue either.) More important, because dopps are primarily used for recording, with limited repertoires of reactive routines, when called on to respond or engage, they do so in the manner most efficiently and predictably *you*: a mirror I found increasingly discomfiting, no, abominable, when tasked with a pair of them *down there*. Weeks before the end. Or before we "abandoned" her: by sundown of the first year, we'd slipped outside communication range with earth.

Starlog no. 1.000001[b]. Where were we? Oh, yes ... the ship. At some point, the über-rich decided to build *down*, bury themselves deeper and deeper underground. Hedging their bets, so to speak. The Heart of B— was a major access point for one such exclusive community, among the most important on the east coast of America's different states. The third concentric ring taking in a wide corner of the park, and the interior ring of pear trees around the fountain and Civil War monument, the crust ... no, the filled-in part, between pockets of nearly lethal air above and caverns of gold underneath, where I engaged in my *top clearance* work, was what would wind up this ship, so it's surpassing strange, even over these heterodimes, to witness the Plaza's prospect with the remains of a park behind, to begin speaking about devastation or what's intact, because the first thing you notice, or I do, did, every time I take it in, is that it's the *exterior of our ship*. A spaceship, in fact or if you will: an escape pod hatched out of our final days, a long-distance traveler for a time and only now trapped in the fickle embrace of these twin moons near the polyp-planet of Nodab[IV]. In the future, it is what it is, but I can't bring myself to look at what it is or isn't, even by remote . . . the discordance affects me in ways it's unhealthy to describe. "Night" being ninety-nine hours away. Take one down, pass it around, ninety-eight hours until sleep prevails. (And yet I keep to maybe one *one-hundredth* of my fellow-travelers' entrainment cycles.) One of these days I'll stop tapping out obsolete terms like *one of these days*. I'm learning, but slowly. Back on earth I thought I was a hare, at least up until my forties. The fact that I was a Lacanian had something to do with it, I suppose. I rushed about making a reputation for myself, obtaining the right sorts of credentials and patients, in a word, overachieving. With sessions rarely lasting more than ten minutes, I was able to squeeze a lot of important people in. In America, I helped make Lacanian analysis the choice of the busy professional: venture capitalists, politicians, media tools. I helped them enter into the game, to discover their true desires undressed like red-faced ingénues, but I never got to that ... that formal *purification* myself. Back on earth I wasn't a hare, I had just found a way to skip the drudge-work, not cheating, not exactly, just cutting corners down to size, practicing pretenses in mirrors angled deliberately to reflect me bigger or glibly engorged. For example I had a natural or God-given aptitude for hypnosis, but I never worked on honing the skill, in fact I was ashamed of it, I felt like a hack performing a parlor game harking back to the disreputable origins of our profession. Besides earning me a place of no small authority on board, I see from my future perspective how little these seemingly large things mattered. In fact, I have doubts as to whether they existed at all, using the term more or less as we did, when we existed, if at all, back on our doomed planet. It took a while for me to switch from over- to underachiever. Now I see I was a tortoise all along, and I've learned to embrace that fact while arguing the "tortoise disposition" as universal precondition for humankind's final 467, while we continue our search for a new planet, our resettlement due any time now. That last sentence is mostly lies, and the term *argue*, while perfectly valid in certain respects, is grossly misleading in others. The discordance I hasten to add, exists between the notional imperative of this captious star system or *outer space* in general, and the place I once knew as *home*, side by side, even coming into contact, touching fingertips.

Stardate datastore 822.0002. Not being able to read these entries back has become a problem. A few of my fellow-travelers decided I'm to blame for *the slow ones*, as they call them, which is true or true enough: it was more than a few. As for blame, I merely accelerated a process that would have occurred anyway or (much more likely) taken them only part way, fluctuating between diverging SCN-periods, the violence of loss competing with violent dementia . . . I gave them an alternative. Both *gave* and *alternative* are true enough, but not when put in the same sentence together. But I could sympathize with the crew's confusion. My fellow-travelers. Yes, I'm still liking that. Living in the future is very confusing. I know all about it. The daily gagging on dialectic frequencies, Hegel in the media room, Castor in the morning mirror waking me at six sharp, but six what? What? Not o'clock, certainly. Later that weekend (a Memorial holiday), I track them all down. One by one, here I come. In this task, I have the advantage of still being sane. If that sounds a bit sinister, understand that I was in much greater peril from them than they were, are, will be from me. Be that as it may, it was time to start listening again. "I tried my damnedest to talk the cat out of the tree, but it wouldn't come down," Johnson was telling me. "Wonderful," I murmured. "What do you mean, 'wonderful'?" asked Johnson, who switched genders when he decelerated, or I did him. Early days yet, early suspicions. "I mean now we're getting somewhere. You're telling me something I don't already know. Is that okay?" "I guess . . ." "I can't help you if I can't understand you." "You're the head-carver." "And why do you think the cat wouldn't come down when you talked to it?" "It didn't trust me! Of course." "Ah," I said. It always came down to trust with them. They were like children who needed to be led back to sleep. With Genevieve, it's different . . . it's the *ship* she's frightened of, more than of me it seems, I don't really rate with her. No, she actively dislikes me. I have my reasons, arguable though they may be, but the ship has whims all its own. According to her, that's the only way to describe them. No, my own theory is terrifying enough: Castor has beamed its black-hole insurrections *into* our ship, stalled or in flux between instability and instability. Anyway, I *think* this is what I think.

In the future, I am less sure of myself. Not sure I think or that it's "I" who does the retailing, therefore—what? Does she understand yet that I can see her?

Log no. 1010101 (two haunted transitions later). I had Barry the IT guy show me how to sever select homodime monitors and screens from the nucleus without damaging the ship or the divisions of labor that kept us alive within its thoughts, so to speak, and then I decelerated him superfast. In theory, I needed to wipe the ship's dataforms of any trace of my activities, but only in theory. Without a proper interface, or any interference from the ship itself, I was on my own . . . Barry was perfectly safe. He'd be "out of phase" until it came time for the great awakening: landfall or my anticipated demise, in whichever order. His (their) slowness is quite disturbing to watch, I admit, hence the panicky talk about *slow ones*. But the fact was, on or within the particular *meta*-earth I'd designed for him, Barry was living life to its putative fullest. They all are. To an uninformed observer, it might seem like a scary parlor game, but to them it's the real thing. That simple truth punches me in the face every day. Their almost *too* expressive faces have become my weather, the way the climate splinters inside the ship, room by room, compartmentalized so as not to get compromised. The biochemical processes I term "deceleration" (rather, my efforts to *accelerate* the ongoing deceleration) began as if by accident: as always, I was seeking to forestall the dementia with Lewy bodies that posed an increasing threat *up here*, the more time went by. Only after weeks into the third year of continuous treatment did I realize that the ameliorators and enhancers I'd generically prescribed (glucose-boosters, souped-up Profiderall and the alpha-through-gamma cholines for stability, performance and autodrive) were having a "paradoxical" effect on a sizable proportion of the crew, myself included. Disorganized speech (the symptom of greatest interest to me, naturally) and fluctuating pronunciations. Recurring visual hallucinations, particularly in those suffering Lewy bodies, macular degeneration, or lesions on the calves of the forebrain. In such cases, the patient will have trouble distinguishing TV images and recorded sounds from his or her "real" environment. If unchecked, this *meta*-reality will often gain ground, even predominating. Drowsiness, lethargy, variable alertness. Depression and sudden rages. Even as we witnessed an uptick in these symptoms, the family resemblance to the narrow-bore senilities being acute, no, astute, no, acute, the effects of basic treatments *down there* only made the dementia worse, while accentuating the attendant motor symptoms, including two I knew all too well, *bradykinesia* and *saltatory tremors*. At first I viewed this as a "paradoxical" side effect, undermining the efficacy of any treatment *up here*. Or did the symptoms relate to our sleep/wake entrainment, as the cocommanders suspected? Perhaps, but it was hardly fair to blame me. Moreover, blaming me *either way*. "Either way," said cocommander Roos, "it's your department. You better start making sense of this pretty soon, or ..." He didn't need to finish: otherwise. I brought him out with a signal from early childhood: "High chair," I said. "I appreciate your honesty," I told him as he swung his feet off the couch, flicking his salt-and-pepper ponytail out of the collar I'd carefully tucked it into. "That felt longer than ten minutes," he responded. Could a dopp do any better? "Wonderful!" I replied, "that means the therapy's working. I'll have answers for you and Terry soon."

Stardate session no. 00002012. As sympathetic ear, I was becoming all ear: "I used to work a thirteen-hour shift at the farm," Harry Newton said, "then I came home and watched three hours of TV. These shows didn't make sense of the days, exactly, but they weren't so far apart either." He was the first I practiced on, the ship's number two (three if you count the cocommanders twice), an extremely suggestive patient, but a bullet of a man as a "civilian," respected and feared immodestly. He had a little sideline going in crew "sobriety and morale," and was a natural supporter of full-crew entrainment, having done a stint on a nuclear submarine. Naturally. They'd been basic protocol for artificial environments since the '60s ... secret tortoise that I was, I administered them with due diligence ... even though no study *down there* had lasted more than a decade, at least nothing with a scientific methodology. (Opportunities for subtle growth pushed *administration* into *orchestration*: after the week's first century passed, I made the cycles as variable as possible.) No scientists, but I remember an interview Phil set up for me with two ponytailed performance "art/ists" a few years before the art world ended: a couple who'd been observing a 49-hour sleep/wake cycle for over sixteen years (their calendar), mostly on public display. They'd occupied a variety of homemade "environments," in out-of-the-way storage or water closets in public museums, in downtown and uptown galleries, in the storefronts of real estate changing hands or leases, in both for- and nonprofit consortiums, using video setups to tune themselves out from their skimpy audience share, sometimes visible *only* on mediating screens. Their present room, walls daubed in cryptochrome, contained a single continuous tone that to me sounded like the first half or note of a siren, a car alarm, something of that nature, listening being balanced on the edge of a knife. Phil, who accompanied me, seemed impressed, and that made me wonder . . . otherwise, no. High pitch or low note, it never varied, stopped, got louder or softer, although it changed depending on the orientation of one's head (the ears posted on either side). It made me more aware of my ears, I think, than ever before. The room seemed larger but at the same time the siren seemed too large for the room, claustrophobia dawning even as the walls breathed out. The pair of them were stone deaf and extremely hostile. We were told they could hear fine so long as the siren/note was present . . . no, I remember, it was a test pattern. The guy looked like he wanted to punch one of us, Phil or me, but couldn't decide who. Despite high expectations, I didn't get much out of the meeting, although I took note of both their *saltatory tremors* and the *bradykinesia*.

*　*　*

Stardate *Isurvivedtheattack*. During the long night of our first century out, the cocommanders fluttered between spur and distraction, covetous as a brace of moths. Now whenever one of them becomes aware of me, he or she will try to murder me. It's that simple. Like the rest. I don't blame them, won't say I wouldn't do the same, etc., but I do have good reason for feeling defensive, always anticipating evil and their slow labors to destroy me. Terry grew up on a farm on the northern Pennsylvania border, pretty near where I was from: "I don't like the hogwash you've been feeding us," she said angrily. "Go on," I encouraged her. I was a little bit in love with Terry. Or I could've been, I suppose, if I allowed myself, if I had anything left over to love with. Listen to me. "Why are you preventing us from being angry?" she'd asked, in the half hour of our first year out. "Don't you think people have a right to feel anger in this situation?" I was impressed by her acuity, and she was beautiful, of course: large, avocado-skinned, with her long black hair tied into a cumbrous ponytail at the base of her neck. "Who, me?" But she wasn't buying. Then I tried: "Rights, now *that's* an interesting question." Nope. "I want you to cut it out, whatever you're doing." When *Terry* issued an order, it was always "I." Roos, on the other hand, favored "we," meaning him and Terry, though possibly a more nebulous consociation. "Doesn't *everybody* have a right to a safe environment?" I asked. "Doesn't that trump everything else? I'll show you the numbers, but it's not a *philosophical* question so much as dire necessity. Talk to Roos. He'll see things my way." "I don't want to dispute this with you," she said. Unpleasant *and* unnecessary: the logical thing was to split them into two cohorts, placebo and treated patients, with the latter covering a range of regimens, at least in theory. In practice, there was too much for one person to do, to try out too many variables. And at that point *up here*, I didn't have quite the authority I obtained later once the numbers one, two, three, four, five, and six (seven if you count the co-commanders twice) were incapacitated. Well before I began to apply stealth-hypnotics to protocol variables. Unpardonable? I've had to defend myself against the charge of playing God so often I've gotten used to the invidious comparison: no . . . the latitudes of space are too wide for this sort of talk, our indwelling too narrow. My role is oversight. Judas goat at worst. I'd known regret, known about it, had a few.

* * *

Logstar *lost argument #23*. In time I understood that the "paradoxical" side effects of treatment were, in fact, primary, no, primal, impinging upon the true mind/body synthesis that (for some reason) the earth's ionosphere had shielded us from. In other words: *up here* our bodies take precedence over mind, so that right off the bat (over time) the crew became all body, their minds weak appendages, mere *Lewy body deceptions* in a sense. Functionally useless. This insight took me far. It carried me, in effect, into the future, where we stayed for an idle vacation from care, they in their invidious I-won't-say realities (not full-fledged, although the *meta*-earths did allow free will to *sort* events within a chosen place/safe STC), me in contemplation of my enchanted childhood. Each deceleration involves more than a formula, each formula the key to unlocking a *meta*-earth. An entire world, if by world, etc. "Hogwash"? I was singlehandedly building the Promised Land, or a Babel ... "either way," no small achievement. "Go on," I encouraged Terry. The rest was the same, the complaints quite unfair from my perspective. From hers, who knows? I took her deeper under, so I could focus on other patients (in fact they'd all pretty much evolved from *patients* to *subjects*). In the future, my words will catch up with me, by which I mean actions. It was proving my busiest week in a long, long time. I watched and listened as buried suspicions and resentments rose to their variable surfaces, estimating how much time I had left with each subject. By this point, nearly everybody was under one form of hypnotic suggestion or another: also about the time when I hit on the idea of the *meta*-earths. Like all dreamers, I was something of a schemer. I started using hypnosis to find out where the dangers for me lay, reasonably enough, but then I realized it was speeding up their Lewy body activity. A formidable moral paradox: at least *up here*. I'd subdivided the *placebites* into two further categories, patient travelers and impatient travelers, and already could see the need for more subdivisions on the horizon. It does no good, not being able to take notes. Given my experience with hallucinogens *down there* ("bad trip," in the parlor games of the time), I didn't allow them near the creation of the *meta*-earths. Dementia was wild card enough. The *meta*-earthly evacuations went slow, slowly because . . . well, it took Lacan nearly thirty years to be banned from the Psychoanalytical Society. That's pretty doggone slow. And I'd discovered something *down there*, as a mistaken hare, about science's place in the world. The politics was just as hard as the science, if not harder. With science you have a methodology, so you can relax some of the time. Politics is all improvise, improvise. The essential ones, I told myself with regard to my moral paradox, but that, as it turned out, with no *reality check*, soon included everybody. "Go on," as I myself might say. Have done.

Stardate datastore 822.00012sub-basement. "Meanwhile," Terry replied (see entry above), "we're all dependent on you staying sane." "Of course!" I said, shocked. "You're the cocommander, I would have thought you'd absorbed that fact by now. I'm *indispensable*." Terry muttered something. "What's that?" I was frightened of their intelligence, where their ideas came from, where the slow articulations whereof would lead: against me, I was certain, and up hard, but how, how hard, *that* I was too quick to comprehend or they too slow ... it was all too elaborate somehow: the way items or images in rapid sequence are often perceived as simultaneous, especially when a variety of senses are stimulated. Not to mention the interactive variables to "confuse" them (*synesthesia*). The first *meta*-earths were impoverished affairs compared to what I've been able to achieve in the future. At first they resembled art installations, each occupied by a single performer, inhabitant or (closer to the truth) *personification* of the *meta*-earth. Plenty of monitors with entrainment entertainment: severely retarded analog footage, super-8, early vohs, even 16-millimarkers, blown out and dealing eight measly frames a second, no, in the future, *up here*, paradox is primary. Think antithesis: *eight seconds a frame!* Think about that for a second (or eight). A life lived eight seconds a frame! Many lives! That's what I saw, a hare turned tortoise of the future. I would slow the spin of our poor old globe by replaying memories brought aboard from *down there* (my own footage mainly, it's not what you think, I had no choice) so as to pin each subject/shipmate without struggle to his or her place on it, a county in some habitable, habit-forming country. I'd like to read that back for tone, if only I could. Like an installation, each of these compartments did, does, would signify its own earth, a *meta*-earth, for putative infinity. To be honest, I'm not sure the quality of installation mattered to my decelerated fellow-travelers. Insofar as I could track them (as one might a weather system, given the infernal *laissez-faire* assistance of the ship), I could see no significant variations between those in the HoJo *meta*-earths, so to speak, and those in the Hiltons. To remove any chance the ship might introduce a network, I've kept as much as I could off the mainframes, but there's a limit to even my inventiveness. I just wish they would quit blaming me. It's universal, it's boring and it's very destructive, even self-destructive, from their point of view, since I have effectively voted myself their caretaker, if by, etc. I'm pretty positive I figure in most of their *meta*-earths, despite my best efforts to *autocorrect* these spiteful tendencies, as a local *daemon*, a bad wind, a witch doctor or some purely temporary mistake of a deity. Hence the accumulation of so many "false earth" scenarios within their rooms, or *meta*-earths. I wish they would stop. I mean, honestly . . . why flatter me?

Log no. 6643466¹/₂. That first month of decades, we pecked like hungry birds at the *solid ground* that had gone long before we'd left it for an idea of posterity in the stars, or a civilization. From my by-no-means-secure perch, I took note of how big concepts and basest needs fused in times of utmost crisis. So much confirmed when it was *almost* the end: two checks from mate. Dear old cancer-ridden earth, filling up its pockets with dead air. I remember how hazy the atmosphere around the *fame pockets* got, if by hazy one means greasy, how they soiled the overbearing sunlight, heat that felt caused by the haze rather than vice versa. I remember the *fame riders*: sports extremists who claimed they could ride in and out of the pockets using elaborate grappling, pulley and eventually rocket apps, none successfully, if by, etc. I remember the panic that swept over me the day our communication devices stopped working, when our animate and inanimate records proved hopelessly corrupt, incapable of sustaining a single *thought*—a word—much less coherent memories. The apocalypse we'd somehow visited on ourselves, and how somehow won. When past and present both became inconceivable, what choice did we have but to enter *The Future*? At the time, even outer space seemed more conceivable to me, to us, if only for the inconceivable present, its paradox contemporary with our own paradoxical existences so inconceivable we couldn't draw a line between *then* and *now*, *now* and *when*. It simply wasn't possible. In the City of B—, the first jolt out of the apathy of the present: I'd slept through the actual (activating) moments of impact, as did most New Yorkers who work days. While those who happened to be awake reported feeling something in interviews on the local news, the "something" proved elusive or incommunicably unique. To my eyes, they were making themselves believe, creating ego-objects so that the extraordinary-but-faraway events mirrored their own reality. A meteor shower on the other side of the planet. One or a group had knocked out Pyongyang. Only that wasn't the worst. I heard experts talking about the entire peninsula "capsizing" (they were careful to put quotes around this term but the effect was the same), kicking up a daisy chain of tsunamis. Japan, gone. Still, we believed that would be the worst. By three that afternoon, we'd lost all communication and storage capacities. A feeling of unreasoning panic set in, slowly . . . but in a sense very fast. A red *Voice*-box conducted into the upper atmosphere, in a matter of seconds: twenty-one, before it was out of sight, I'd timed it, the last thing I *did* time, in a sense. "It was like I'd pulled a muscle," the last of my patients *down there* told me, rotating his shoulders, Peter Quinn, so as to demonstrate. "But it was like everybody there with me had as well. The same fucking muscle, pardon my French." "We've been over this before," I said, "don't you think it's time to return to the present?" Of course, I'd also said all this before. I wasn't paying attention, distracted by the news of the day and then the sight of that voice-box ascending out of sight in under half a minute.

I was trying to think of what it could mean. Nothing good. Quinn was dropping pennies into my tropical fish hologram, which I found plenty irritating. "That's because you're not helping me! I mean if I wanted to hear 'just forget about it,' I wouldn't walk two hours each way through some pretty sketchy neighborhoods right now to meet with you, I'd ask my fiancée . . . you know?" *Plop!* I believe this tic was his (possibly unconscious) method of preventing me from repeating his last thought, so as to gain time, and to the degree that it worked, I remained silent, I swiveled in my chair and said

Starlog *something with a date in it.* To disrupt the routines, I need to establish them first, that's how this form of analysis works: to surprise the unconscious, catch it on the fly, so to speak, flagrantly revealing its true desire. Ordinarily, I liked Peter. Like most human "bomb-sniffers," whether altered at birth or in their teens, he had an air of fertile aggrievement that is the provenance of men (and they are *always* men) who have betrayed themselves. Those who have only themselves to blame and know it. Let me be very clear: if I go, they all go, everybody knows that, it's my burden, I alone had the power-personality to stand up to the strain, straining under its impossible weight, a tortoise who'd once strained to be a hare. *Down there*, the official rumor was earth had been knocked out of its orbit . . . and now here I am attempting to establish communication with the remains of whatever's there or was, teletapathic. I wander into the weightless part of the ship to get a haircut. Looking into the mirror of the past, I realized it's been that long. In his *meta*-earth, Frank the Barber is teaching his apprentice (who resembles a paranoid, low-IQ personality I evaluated *down there*) how to employ the hedge-clippers. In hers, the widow Terry is heading into B— from her farm. It was meant to be a dairy farm, but they kept all of three cows along with some pigs, chickens and water fowl, and even these Terry had a hard time keeping in good health. The lines were down, and she had to ride in. The air was nippy. On the other side of the globe (now Nicholson), Roos has a different wife with a boy and stepdaughter. Also a hobby: he's putting the finishing touches on a miniature ship before making it swoon into an empty bottle. This will take him about seven years on the last day, by my endogenous watch. Minutes, if he were to be phased back to *The Future*. It all sounds complicated, but it wasn't, and once I'd split them up even inside their *meta*-earths (to be on the safe side), I didn't have much to do except to monitor, like I "monitored" the ship or the readouts of the void and its moon- or world-sized interruptions outside and all around. Yes. I never looked. No. I looked once and never looked again. No pillars of salt for me. The idea of black holes inside this immense black hole we travel through (used to, will again, but not now, in my purely *temporary* future-present) is so ridiculous it makes me laugh, almost. In theory, I would be able to replay all of them, of course, to speed the recordings up to my level would be a simple matter, slow or accelerate as need be, I'd have to bypass the ship some more, and introduce a playback function. But in theory it's possible. Why? Because *they can see her.* They can see Genevieve without the windows of the monitors I require. The only explanation is she (and Muncie) live in two STCs simultaneously, perhaps more . . . operating between them as conducting media.

III. SYNTHESIS

By and by, the thread holding it is invisible, and it twitches the larval creature upwards. Whenever the wind lifts the branch, it curls up like a scrap of paper in fire. A caterpillar lowered like bait from the low branch of a sapling. Pansies splash the tall grass. Burrweeds, ferns, shrubs. I don't choose to but get too close to her and wake on planet Nod. I liked the climate there. Not this primordial gravy, but the moral climate . . . I'd gone to school in Bearden, several lifetimes ago, college, and then I stuck around for a PhD. We should have listened to the "natives," but we were kids back then. I did. I did listen, that is, but that only encouraged me, I was prone to carelessness back when I thought myself a hare. Genevieve and Muncie have opened a channel with me and with them, *the slow ones*, possibly transporting them back to earth for a spell, merging and then emerging on the other side, however they managed to suppress it, wherever we are. *These* were Bearden's ghosts, like the natives always claimed: a two-way channel of communication. An *earth* channel. The *ghosts* of my past were in fact my future *fellow-travelers*, the ones I'd helped survive, each acting out his or her pleasant routines in the *meta*-earths, now, sometimes, back on our old ideal of earth as well. Where I'd give my right hand or left soul to be. We squeezed as much "atmosphere" as we could out of the old girl, and sent her into space, knowing the risks. Once I realized Genevieve could be a *conduit* back to a past I had been groping towards without understanding, heedless as a plant, I knew I needed to contact her, whatever the cost, to merge if necessary but to emerge out the other side: that's what was important. The natives of Bearden were right on target about their ghosts. Everything is all-at-once, but one gets used to it: old memories, vivid pockets opening everywhere, finally even reaching the "safe neighborhoods" of B—, picking up sidewalk trash at first and then sending whole buildings into the bottomless air, ventilating them floor by floor, revealing the sedimentary strata of apartments, tenements, towers, brownstones. It feels as if, all together, we collaborated on something really, really terrible. Our true desire. The end of the world, of our world, *our* and *the* being interchangeable (more or less) in this instance. She came to us, to me, in the emptiness of my loneliness, little more than a girl, relative to me. At the bottom of all moral quandaries, always and everywhere, is desire. If Genevieve was in fact a pioneer, an early *outrider* from the 1974 ghost-rip, then I should have pulled away, but I couldn't: *they* were the only ones waiting for me. Slowed to waxy stillness, moving only when I wasn't around or looking elsewhere. Otherwise. While waiting, holding hands, while I had mine behind my back, thinking, this is it. When I watched her as she stepped between devices relating her image to the monitor at hand, I knew that I (like *them*) could never be complete, never be at one with my fate, without that perilous nostalgia ... yet I kept my distance. Why? My scruples make no sense to me. Our spiritual guide aboard ship, Frank Denby, the person most likely to oppose me, especially if he was a "good" man (and Frank was), wasn't a threat because he was so terribly passive. I suppose he'd say "resigned." I'll stay with what I have. He believed the Cartesian proof of God the best offered, even to this day, because it "started the farthest back." He was interested in what I thought happened to dialectical materialism in a world *without material*. I corrected the many errors in his question, but he hung in there. He never called it "the ship," it was always "the world," with variations like our *new* or *present* world. Always world. Back then I worried about these subdivisions in language preferences, not realizing how helpful they would be in my compartmentalization of 467 distinct *meta*-earths. Client or patient? I realized he regarded me as a *client*: the same way I regarded my own patients. He believed the universe to be inherently moral at its core, and that as long as we had life support, we'd do fine, we'd adapt, the ship would drift or be very slowly dragged towards the Great Attractor. That's all he said: nobody had tried that tactic on me. "What are you doing?" he asked. It was effective. I was frightened of his opinion, I admit it. That's the big difference between us, I decided: *I* still feel I have a lot to do. Even though he was only eight years older, I regarded him as a surrogate father: in my favor he looked a good deal older than his actual age, while I still looked young. Then why do I feel so guilty when I think about him? I gave Frank a good life, if by life one means a room-sized *meta*-earth, and he was able to choose the sort of talk that pleased him most, in that sociable, serene, almost philosophical environment. The paradox of placement into the *meta*-earths (like the paradox of everything else *up here*) meant I often had to reverse settled characteristics of each occupant. The routine makes us all feel better, for a little while. "What's that?" I asked. "Get rid of me," Frank replied, "and how will you ever know you aren't just floating around infinity as the result of some individual fame pocket?" "I'm not a solipsist," I added. As a matter of fact, what I derived from a cosmic linkage outraging every coincidence except the universal one of *tedious expiation* (the reorientation of a single human entry, my own) was that the universe is manifestly moral at its core, if not benign as my good friend Frank believed, but rather framed on an ethical system older than humankind, built into the big bang, in a sense, and that I was being thrust back into my *true desire*, so as to make amends. Not that I mattered, I thought, and maybe I didn't, maybe I did. To be born again! Only *this* entry you'll need to read from the bottom up.

ACKNOWLEDGMENTS

"The Melting Giant" quotes the Beatles' "Hey Jude" (Lennon/McCartney) from *Hey Jude* on page 46. "Bitter Angel" quotes Smog's "What Kind of Angel" (Bill Callahan) from *Julius Caesar* on page 65. Quote on page 98 of "Box with Stories Inside" is from "The Summer Farmer" by John Cheever, *Collected Stories*, with plot lines from a number of stories summarized on pages 98 and 99 (others referenced obliquely in "Tom Thimble.") "Taken/Not Taken" lifts plot elements and lines from Saral Waldorf's "Stage Directions for Screaming," with the author's permission. The "nectar of self-awareness" on page 148 of "A Visit to the Second Floor" is taken from a title by George Franklin. Catastrophe sections of "Tom Thimble" adapt language from Daniel Defoe's *Journal of the Plague Year*. Quote in "Guiding Lights" on page 269 adapted from Karl Marx, *The Eighteenth Brumaire of Louis Bonaparte*. General idea of "slow ones" in "Between Moons" and other stories inspired by Adolfo Bioy Casares's *A Plan for Escape*.

Deepest thanks to Jonathan for making the leap—*twice!* Who does that? Deepest thanks to Lars for his astute advice and edits, to Ana and Tiger for their continuing inspiration, to Dara for all her support, to my mother for her lifelong mentoring. Special thanks to Chris, without whose friendship and support I wouldn't be writing this at all. Deep gratitude to Meredith, Andrew, Lauren, and Maya, who offered key feedback, edits, and strategies during the early stages. Thanks to John R. and the folks in class, who gave "Fetch" its current ending. Dedicated to Helen, who read many of these stories many times, nourished my intuitions about their strange affinities, and brought every one of them into port. The debts can never be repaid.

MAREK WALDORF

was born in Washington DC and grew up in various places: Idi Amin's Uganda, coup-wracked Thailand, punk-era England, and apartheid-encircled Lesotho, but primarily Binghamton, New York— the inspiration for Bearden County. He currently lives in Astoria, New York, where he writes grants for non-profits like Girls Write Now. His first novel, *The Short Fall*, is available from Turtle Point Press.